Mystery on Maui

Nancy caught her breath as George's surfboard catapulted through the air. Where is she? Nancy thought anxiously. Then she spotted her. George had been thrown off the board and was in the water.

Her arms churned furiously as she fought her way through the waves back to the board, but it seemed to Nancy that her friend had disappeared under a whitecap.

When George reappeared, she was farther out in open sea. As Nancy watched helplessly, George was tossed high by one rolling wave, then crashed down with the next. Her head disappeared from view again.

Nancy felt an electric shock run through her body as she realized what was happening. George would drown if Nancy didn't get help fast!

Nancy Drew
Mystery Stories

Available from Simon & Schuster

DREW 143

MYSTERY ON MAUI

CAROLYN KEENE

Aladdin Paperbacks
New York   London   Toronto   Sydney   Singapore

This book is a work of fiction. Any references to historical events, real people, or real locales are used fictitiously. Other names, characters, places, and incidents are the product of the author's imagination, and any resemblance to actual events or locales or persons, living or dead, is entirely coincidental.

First Aladdin Paperbacks edition May 2002
First Minstrel edition June 1998

Copyright © 1998 by Simon & Schuster, Inc.
Produced by Mega-Books, Inc.

ALADDIN PAPERBACKS
An imprint of Simon & Schuster
Children's Publishing Division
1230 Avenue of the Americas
New York, NY 10020

Printed in the United States of America

20 19 18 17 16 15

ISBN-13: 978-0-671-00753-9
ISBN-10: 0-671-00753-X
0212 OFF

Contents

MYSTERY ON MAUI

1

Fun in the Sun

"Heads up, Nancy!" George Fayne's voice rang
out over the sound of the crashing surf. "This
one's awesome, and it's got your name on it."

Nancy Drew waved at her friend and lined up
her surfboard to catch the crest of the huge wave
that was rolling in. "I've got it, George," she
called.

After paddling with her arms to launch the
board into the wave, Nancy rose to her feet and
easily caught her balance. She skimmed lightly
across the eight-foot swell to the spot where the
wave flipped forward. Then she rode the inside
curl until it ran up onto the beach with a foamy
crash.

"That was the best ride of the day!" Nancy

shouted to George, who had just cruised in behind her. "Let's get Bess to try some surfing."

"Fat chance." George's tone was teasing but affectionate. "That would mean she'd actually have to get off her beach blanket."

Bess Marvin, George's cousin, preferred to spend her recreational time watching sports from the comfort of the sidelines. George was just the opposite. Lean and active, she loved to participate in any kind of sport. Both girls were Nancy's best friends.

"Did I hear someone say *fat?*" Bess's voice drifted across the sand. George's petite cousin raised her blond head from the blanket where she was sunbathing. "I hope you're not talking about me, 'cause we're on vacation here in Hawaii all week, and I refuse to think about dieting."

"Oh, too bad, Bess, because I just found out about this great Hawaiian pineapple diet," George said, shaking the seawater from her dark brown curls. "It's guaranteed to work, or else you get a free plane ticket to return to Hawaii any time—"

George stopped just in time to duck a wadded-up towel that Bess had lobbed at her.

"Don't worry Bess, we weren't talking about you," Nancy said, lowering herself into a beach

2

chair. "Besides, you know you look fantastic in that suit."

Bess was wearing a white one-piece bathing suit that set off her trim figure.

"Thanks. You look good, too, Nancy," Bess replied. "I noticed a few guys checking you out as you were riding that last wave. There was one guy *I* noticed. He was riding an aqua surfboard. He's cute—and a great surfer, too."

"I saw him," George said. "He's the one who did that amazing air flip. I've never seen anyone do that before, except on TV."

"Well, I guess this beach is 'Surfer Central' this week," Nancy said. "Anyone big in the surfing world should be here for the competition."

Nancy, Bess, and George had arrived on the Hawaiian island of Maui a few days before the start of the island's biggest surfing competition. The contest had drawn surfers from all over the world.

The three friends were visiting for a week at the home of Danny Takemura, one of Nancy's friends who had spent his junior year of high school in River Heights. Nancy and Danny had become good friends during that year, and they'd stayed in touch ever since as E-mail pen pals.

The three girls were sprawled on a beach near Honolua, on the northwest coast of Maui. The white-sand beach formed a long, graceful crescent between two hills. It was divided in two by a long wooden pier. Dotted with graceful coconut palms, the hills and beach framed a sparkling blue jewel of a bay. Right then the bay was rolling with ten-foot waves.

"Don't look now, but there's an aqua surfboard heading our way," George said.

"What?" Bess glanced in the direction that George was looking. Two tall guys were approaching. One of them was holding an aqua-colored surfboard.

Bess bent her head toward Nancy. "Oh my gosh, Nan—it's *him*," she whispered urgently. "The cute one. I think I'm going to die. How do I look?"

"Pretty good—for a person who's about to die," Nancy replied, suppressing a laugh. "Hey, that's Danny with your surfer dude, and something tells me we're about to be introduced."

"Hey, you three," Danny called out his greeting. His voice rose pleasantly in the rolling Hawaiian accent that was common among those who had grown up on the islands.

"I want you to meet my buddy, Josh," Danny said. "He and I have known each other since third grade. Even so, he's still a *malihini*. That means he's a newcomer in Hawaiian."

"Yeah, well, I had to come over from California to save you islanders from losing all your surfing

4

competitions," Josh said as he playfully punched his friend. "Josh Brightman," he added, smiling down at Nancy and Bess. "I'm the polite one."

Josh was broad shouldered and deeply tanned, with a shock of sun-bleached golden brown hair that spilled over his forehead and curled in back almost to his shoulders. The outer edges of his hazel eyes were lightly creased—from a life spent squinting into the sun, Nancy surmised.

"I saw you out there on the water," Bess said, the faintest sign of a blush rising to her cheeks. "You were really good."

"Josh is a legend among us surfers," Danny said. "He's hands-down favored to win the Golf Coast Surf-Off that starts this Saturday."

"Golf Coast? That's what they call this western part of Maui, isn't it?"

"I guess you really did read all the guidebooks I sent you, Nancy," Danny said with a chuckle.

"Golf Coast is also the name of a sports store that's big in Hawaii and California," Josh said. "They're the primary sponsor of the contest this week. It's a big event for them in many ways. They're adding a line of surfboards, and this is a great way to let people know about it."

Danny rubbed his hands together with anticipation. "Just think, Josh, only three more days till you win that prize money—seventy-five thousand big ones."

"Seventy-five thousand dollars?" George let out a small gasp.

Josh grinned. "Yeah, it's big money, but I'm not spending it yet. There are a lot of great surfers signed up to compete. Any one of them could win."

"No chance, Josh-o," Danny said, opening the cooler he and the girls had packed back at his house. He pulled out some cans of soda and handed them around. "You've got it nailed. There's no one here who knows the local waters like you do."

"Well, Jo Jo Sergeant and Keiko Mann were favored to win." Josh set down his board and took a soda from Danny. "But both of them had to drop out of the contest pretty suddenly. Tough break for both of them. Jo Jo came from the mainland and Keiko from Japan to compete. They were the two top contenders."

"Why did they drop out?" Nancy asked.

Josh shrugged. "Keiko got really sick all of a sudden—food poisoning, they think—and Jo Jo had an accident and broke a leg. They're both laid up at the motel where all the out-of-town guys are staying. It's not unusual to have last-minute dropouts, but it is kind of weird that the two top guns got knocked out of the running like that."

6

"That sounds like a mystery for you, Nan." George nodded at Nancy.

Nancy jokingly placed her hands on her hips. "This vacation is strictly for R and R—rest and relaxation. No mysteries," she said in a mock-stern voice. "Only fun and sun are allowed all week."

Mysteries and adventure had a way of following Nancy Drew wherever she went. The eighteen-year-old daughter of criminal lawyer Carson Drew had already established a reputation as an excellent detective by solving a number of difficult cases.

"You guys may be here to take it easy," Josh said, "but I've got work to do. I have to sign up for the opening heat at the sponsor's tent. Then I'm going to hit the surf again. Would you like to come along?"

He was greeted with a resounding "yes" from the group.

"I'd love to, but I don't know how to surf," Bess replied uncertainly.

"I'll give you a lesson," Josh offered. He took Bess's hand and helped her to her feet.

Josh and Bess walked a little ahead of the others, talking and laughing as they headed down the beach toward the blue- and white-striped sponsor's tent next to the main pier.

"Bess seems to like Josh," George whispered to Nancy. "I haven't seen her blush like that in a while."

Nancy nodded. "Well, she's right about one thing—he is cute. And he seems nice, too." She paused and glanced out over the ocean.

"I'll bet you're thinking of someone right now," George said.

Nancy gave her friend a little smile. "You're a mind reader, George. I was just thinking how nice it would be to walk along this beach at sunset with Ned."

Ned Nickerson, whom Nancy dated, was attending classes back home at Emerson College. The sight of Bess and Josh having fun made Nancy realize how much she missed Ned's sparkling brown eyes and good sense of humor.

The Golf Coast sponsor's tent was a beehive of activity. Surfers clustered in front of a registration table.

"Be back in a sec," Josh said to his friends as he joined the other surfers at the booth.

Nancy was checking out a display of T-shirts when she sensed that someone was watching her. She turned around and saw a man standing slightly apart from the other surfers. The man, who seemed to be in his early twenties, had a shiny black surfboard and an arrogant look on his

8

bronzed face. He nodded to Nancy without smiling.

"Who's the guy with the black surfboard?" Nancy whispered to Danny when he walked over to join her.

Danny followed Nancy's gaze. "Oh, that's Hank Carter," he said slowly. "We call him the Lone Wolf of Maui. He's a few years older than we are and keeps to himself, even though we all knew him while we were growing up. He's super competitive and gets bent out of shape during a contest like this."

Just then Nancy felt another set of eyes on her, these from a woman with long, silky white blond hair. She was standing next to Hank. The girl shot Nancy a sharp look. She tapped Hank on the elbow to get his attention. He gave Nancy one final glance before turning his attention back to his friend.

"I guess your Hank's no lone wolf when it comes to girls," Nancy commented as she and Danny rejoined their friends outside the tent.

Danny laughed. "Yeah, on that score he's more of what you might call a real lady-killer."

Josh greeted them outside the registration area. He had his surfboard under one arm and his registration forms in his free hand.

"Let's head back to the spot where you were

9

sunbathing," he said. "The surf's a little calmer there, and that would be a better place for Bess's lesson."

A short while later Josh led Bess into the water while Nancy, George, and Danny stretched out on their towels. Nancy took out a selection of local fruit—guava, mango, pineapple, and papaya—from the cooler. "This I have to watch," George said gleefully as Bess took Josh's surfboard. "If only I had a camera."

"If anyone could get Bess out there, it would be Josh," Nancy said. "Look! He actually has her on the board."

Bess was riding the surfboard on her stomach for a while to get the feel of it, Nancy assumed. Then she saw Josh showing Bess how to rise to a standing position.

"She's waiting for a good set of waves," Nancy said with delight. Bess hugged the board for a while, then rose uncertainly to her feet. She raised her arms as if she were on a balance beam, leaning first to one side, then the other.

"Wobbling right . . . then left . . . and forward . . . and back she goes! Tough break for the rookie," George called out like a sports announcer as Bess tumbled backward off the board, directly into Josh's arms.

"Well, at least she had a soft landing," Nancy said with a grin.

Just then Nancy noticed a blur of motion to her left. A scruffy-looking man had emerged from the low-lying brush near a stand of palms. His head was shaved, and he had a stubble of beard. The man sprinted toward the waterline.

"Boy, he's really hotfooting it," Danny commented.

"Yes," Nancy replied. "Why do you suppose—"

To their surprise, the man made a beeline for the spot where Josh's surfboard had drifted to shore. He grabbed the board and hoisted it above his head.

"Look at that," Nancy cried, already on her feet. "That guy's stealing Josh's board. We've got to stop him!"

2

Hot Pursuit

Nancy dug her heels into the soft sand to gain ground on the man who had grabbed Josh's surfboard.

The thief was very fit—and very fast. He covered a lot of ground quickly, even while carrying the bulky board. Nancy had to double her speed to narrow the distance between them.

Once or twice Nancy saw the man glance over his shoulder and abruptly change course. The two now zigzagged directly along the shore toward a rocky breakwater.

"Stop right there!" Nancy shouted as they neared the structure.

The thief hesitated for a second and glanced about for an escape route. As she moved in,

Nancy saw that he had a tattoo that circled his right arm. The design made it look as if a black snake was slithering up the entire length of his arm.

The man heaved Josh's surfboard against a boulder at the base of the breakwater. Then he darted for the nearest line of trees and disappeared from view.

Nancy sloshed through the surf and clambered onto the boulders to retrieve Josh's board. Examining it, she saw that there were some dents along the runner, but the board was basically intact.

Danny and George came running up behind Nancy. "Are you okay?" George asked with a worried expression.

"I'm fine, but I'm not sure about Josh's board. It looks pretty banged up," Nancy replied.

Nancy, George, and Danny headed back to the spot on the beach where they'd left their cooler and chairs. Josh and Bess were waiting anxiously for them, along with a cluster of onlookers who'd been attracted by the commotion.

"We didn't see what happened. We just saw you three suddenly take off down the beach like a pack of dogs chasing a cat," Josh said. He took the surfboard from Nancy. "Thanks for saving my board. I hate to think that you took a risk like that."

Nancy described the man who took the board.

Neither Danny nor Josh could recall seeing anyone who fit that description.

"A snake tattoo winding all the way up his arm? That's too weird." George shook her head. "We'll have to call him the Snake until we find out who he is."

"Snake is a perfect name for a creep like that," Nancy said. "Why do you think someone would steal a surfboard?" She addressed the question to Josh. "Does that happen much?"

"No, this is unusual," Josh replied. "Especially considering that the board is pretty old. It doesn't have any market value, except to me. I call this board Old Magic. I've won so many competitions with it that I can't imagine competing without it. It's kind of a superstition, I guess."

"That's interesting," Nancy said, staring off in the distance.

"I can see the wheels turning behind those blue eyes of yours," George said. "What are you thinking, Nancy?"

"I was remembering what Josh said about those other two top surfers having to drop out of the contest this week because of unusual mishaps," Nancy replied. "And now this Snake guy tries to steal Josh's board."

"You think there could be a connection?" Bess's eyes widened.

"I think it's a possibility," Nancy replied slowly. "Someone could be trying to drive the top surfers away from the contest this week."

"But why?" George looked puzzled.

Nancy shrugged. "That seventy-five-thousand-dollar prize is a lot of money. Maybe someone is trying to better the chances of another surfer. People have been known to commit crimes for a lot less money."

"No way." Josh shook his head. "Surfers don't operate like that. It's proving yourself against the waves that counts—not competing against other surfers. The money is secondary."

"That's the way losers think." A voice cut into the conversation.

Nancy turned to see Hank Carter standing just behind her. Close up, she could see his dark eyes and brooding expression underneath his short-cropped hair. The same girl was with him.

"The judges aren't going to give the prize money to the surfer who tries the hardest. The money goes to the surfer who wins," Hank said to Josh.

"If all you think about is money, then you're the loser, Hank," Josh retorted.

Hank shrugged and glanced down at Josh's surfboard. "Speaking of losing, I saw you blow off your board while you were goofing around in the water," he said with a hint of a smile. "Lucky for

15

you this lovely lady rescued it for you," he added with a sidelong glance at Nancy.

"Come on, Hank. Let's get out of here," the blond girl interjected in an irritated voice. She shot Nancy an icy look.

"All right, Marisa," Hank replied. "Catch you later." He addressed Josh as he left.

Josh grimaced. "Great exit line, 'Catch you later,'" he muttered under his breath. "Let him try. That guy is always trying to get me riled."

"What kind of competitor is Hank?" Nancy asked Josh. "Aside from his being a lousy sport, I mean. Is he a good surfer?"

Josh paused to consider Nancy's question. "Now that Jo Jo and Keiko have dropped out, I would say Hank's my main competition," he replied. "He doesn't have a lot of natural talent, but he makes up for it with discipline and sheer nerve. Hank never gets rattled out there on the waves, which is hard to do when you're staring at a two-story wall of water about to crash down on your head."

"Hank's girlfriend didn't seem too happy," Bess observed.

Josh grinned. "Marisa is kind of a snob—we call her the Ice Princess."

Danny was examining Josh's surfboard. "What do you think, Josh," he asked his friend. "Worth trying to repair her?"

"You bet," Josh ran a hand gently down the board's runner. "A little resin and a once-over with a fiberglass cloth, and she'll be good as new. I can pick up some repair stuff at Ruby's."

"Ruby's?" Nancy asked. "Is that someone's house or someone's store?"

"It's a store," Josh replied.

"Ruby's Place is a surf shop near the fishing marina in Lahaina," Danny added. "It's named after the owner, Ruby Blackwell. She's really cool."

"Mind if I tag along when you go?" Nancy asked. "I'd like to check out the fishing marina. The Snake was wearing what looked like fishermen's clothes. Maybe someone there has seen him before."

"Sure," Josh replied. "Why don't we go now? You're coming, too, Bess?" he asked hopefully.

"Of course," Bess said happily.

Leaving George and Danny behind to surf some more, Nancy and Bess rode in Josh's van to the nearby seaside town of Lahaina. At the center of town, a marina bustled with the activity of sailboats and fishing vessels.

As they looked for a spot to park the van, Josh explained that the town had been settled in the 1800s by a group of New Englanders. "That's why it looks like a quaint East Coast fishing village," he said.

Ruby's Place was nestled among picturesque shops and restaurants that overlooked the marina. As they parked, Nancy could see a group of young surfers hanging out in front of the shop with their boards propped up against the storefront.

"Looks like this is a really popular spot," Nancy commented to Josh as he unloaded his surfboard from the back of the van.

Josh nodded. "We all like to hang here. Ruby's our local celebrity," he explained. "She was a world-class surfer before she quit to open this place."

He lowered his voice as they entered the shop. "She and Hank used to be kind of a team, but they split up a couple of years ago. I don't think he's been serious about anyone since her."

"Josh Brightman, is that really you?" A female voice exclaimed. Ruby Blackwell greeted Josh with hug. "You haven't come here once this month. And what have you done to Old Magic!" she said, eyeing his surfboard.

"Made a mess of her, I'm afraid," Josh replied. "Ruby, I'd like you to meet my friends from the mainland, Nancy and Bess. They're visiting Danny Takemura this week."

Ruby nodded hello to Nancy and Bess. Ruby was every bit the celebrity that Josh had described. Tall and thin, she had a striking face with high cheekbones and a caramel-colored complexion. She wore her jet black hair pulled to one side in a thick braid. Her outfit, a sarong and halter top, made her look like a modern-day Hawaiian princess.

Adorning Ruby's bare midriff was an unusual piece of jewelry—a sparkling navel ring set with tiny red jewels that looked like real rubies.

Josh showed Ruby his damaged board. The young shop owner knelt down to examine it.

"I'm afraid you may not be able to do cutbacks the same even if you repair her, Josh," she said, looking up at him. "I can lend you one of my Stingers for the Golf Coast, if you'd like to try it." She pointed toward a row of sleek, tri-fin surfboards that were displayed on the wall.

Josh smiled and shook his head. "I've heard your Stinger is an amazing new design, but this week I need to ride something tried-and-true."

Josh told Ruby how Nancy had rescued his board. "It would have been a goner for sure, except for her," he said, touching Nancy's arm. "She really hotdogged after that slob and saved the day."

"Good for you, Nancy." Ruby gazed at Nancy with new interest.

Nancy described the would-be thief, including

his snake tattoo. "Have you ever seen anyone around here who looks like that?" she asked Ruby.

Ruby thought for a moment. "No, and I know everybody here in Lahaina," she replied. "He's probably from off-island."

"Nancy's going to help us get to the bottom of everything," Josh said. "Back where she comes from she's helped the police solve lots of crimes."

"I'll let you know if I hear anything," Ruby said.

A beeping noise sounded from the back of the shop. "That's my computer's alarm clock," Ruby said. "I have it rigged up to go off when an E-mail message comes in," she said as she headed for the back.

"I'd like to check around the fishing docks," Nancy said to Josh when Ruby was out of earshot. "I want to see if anyone's seen the Snake around here."

"Good plan," Josh said. He purchased his repair supplies from a clerk at the front counter, and they headed back outside. One of the young surfers in front of the shop greeted them.

"Hey, Josh," the boy said eagerly. "You tried Ruby's Stinger yet? They say that board really rips out there."

Josh gave the kid a thumbs-up sign as he,

Nancy, and Bess headed to his van to stow the board and supplies.

"Amateur surfers think some high-tech new board will make the difference for them out on the waves," he said as he loaded his board into the back of the van. "But it's the quality of the surfer, not the equipment, that counts."

They crossed the street to the marina, where a network of wooden docks extended into the harbor. They passed two fishermen on deck. The two men stood over a plastic tub and poured their morning's catch into it. The silver fish gleamed in the sunlight as they cascaded down.

"Yuck." Bess wrinkled her nose at the odor. "Fish is definitely off the menu for me tonight," she stated.

Nancy's eye was drawn to a big boat that was just docking. Painted along the entire length of the forty-foot vessel was a white shark. The painted shark had its jaws open wide, as if it were about to attack. A sign hanging on the side of the boat said, "Cap'n Frye's Shark Attack! See Gaping Jaws of Death!" in bloodred letters.

"Shark attack?" Nancy read the sign in a puzzled tone. "What's that?"

Josh's expression darkened. "I can't believe that Frye's at it again," he said through clenched teeth. "I thought we shut him down for good last week.

"Russell Frye runs a shark-feeding operation," Josh explained. "Frye and his crew take tourists out to the reef and dump loads of chum—a mixture of meat and fish—into the water to attract sharks. The blood in the chum drives the sharks into a feeding frenzy."

"Isn't that dangerous?" Bess shivered.

"It sure is," Josh replied. "For the sharks as well as people. Because the sharks get used to being fed by people, they have to be killed when they get too close to the beaches."

Josh explained that he had recently led an effort by a local environmental group to shut down the shark-feeding operation. "We got the MPA, the Marine Protection Agency, to clamp down on Frye just last week. And now he's out here again, breaking the law."

A couple of crew members on the boat lowered a small gangplank. Moments later a burly, bearded man emerged on deck and disembarked. He had a sour look on his face. Josh stepped forward.

"Hey, Frye. What's up?" He greeted the captain in a challenging tone.

Frye stopped dead in his tracks and glowered at Josh. "You'd better watch your step, Brightman," he snapped. "I know you and those bleeding-heart fish-huggers were behind that MPA ruling by the state."

"Maybe *you* should watch out, Frye," Josh replied angrily. "I'm sure the authorities would like to know that you're violating the law right now."

"Oh, yeah?" Frye went nose to nose with Josh. Meanwhile, his two crew members silently moved in and closed ranks behind their boss. "You've made a mistake, messing with me," Frye's tone was soft but deadly. "Now you'll learn a lesson."

Frye reached for something long and gleaming at his belt. Nancy felt a pang of fear at what she saw.

Frye's hand was hovering over a large, jagged-edged fishing knife. He didn't seem to be afraid to use it, either!

3

One False Move

Adrenaline coursed through every vein in Nancy's body as she anticipated the captain's next move. Would Frye dare pull a knife on Josh on a crowded dock in broad daylight?

Josh was frozen, staring at Frye's hand poised over the fishing knife. Frye didn't make a move.

"Ever seen a fish that was gutted by one of these?" Frye said in a menacing tone. He tapped the knife's metal handle. "It makes a real mess, believe me."

Nancy steeled herself to help fend off a knife strike by Frye. Behind him, Frye's crew exchanged wary glances. There was a tense moment as they all seemed to hold their breaths, waiting for what would happen next.

Nancy glanced swiftly at Bess. Her friend's hands were trembling slightly.

Stay calm, Bess, Nancy silently urged. This was not the time to panic, she knew.

Frye lunged at Josh. Nancy's foot shot out and back quickly, causing the captain to trip. Frye staggered as he tried to keep from falling.

With arms flailing, he fell sideways over the edge of the dock and landed in the water with a huge splash.

For a second, everyone stared open-mouthed at the sight of Frye thrashing around in the harbor like a wounded sea lion. Then Frye's two crewmen let out a roar of laughter.

Their outburst infuriated Frye, and he let loose a string of insults at his men.

Frye continued to bluster while getting out of the water as Josh and Nancy led a hasty retreat from the scene.

Bess released her tension in a fit of nervous giggles. "That Captain Frye looked so ridiculous when he fell overboard," she said, gasping with laughter.

"Cool move, Nancy," Josh said with admiration. "You made it look like he tripped over his own feet."

"Frye deserved it," Nancy commented. "What a creep."

When they had almost made it back to the van,

they bumped into Ruby Blackwell. She was holding a computer printout in her hand. "Hey, what's going on, you guys?" she asked.

Josh described their run-in with Frye. Ruby shook her head disapprovingly at Josh. "You shouldn't mess with him," she said. "You know as well as I do that Frye can be really dangerous. Just last month he got thrown in jail for fighting."

Josh set his jaw stubbornly. "I could've handled Frye," he muttered. "He's not so tough."

"Oh, yeah? It sounds like you handled him real well." Ruby made a clucking sound with her tongue. "It sounds to me as if you've needed help twice today from your friend Nancy."

Josh sighed. "I guess you're right, Ruby. I should probably learn to pick my battles more carefully. At least my battles with Frye."

"What do you know about Frye?" Nancy asked the shop owner.

"Frye's a *kamaaina*—an islander," Ruby explained to Nancy and Bess. "He and I grew up in the same village near here. Back then he was a bully, too, but he never bothered me or my family. Now, though, he seems to be out of control, so I stay away from him."

Ruby held up the pages in her hand. "I followed you guys from the shop to tell you about this weather bulletin I got. We just pulled it off the Internet," she said, handing the sheet to

Josh. "I'm afraid it may be bad news for the competition."

Nancy peered over Josh's shoulder to read the weather advisory. A major tropical storm was bearing down on the island, it said. The storm would likely hit on Saturday—the same day that the Golf Coast Surf-Off was scheduled to begin.

"How bad do you think the storm will be?" Nancy asked them.

"Bad enough," Josh replied simply. "They've already issued warnings for small craft and swimmers," he added, tapping the printout.

"It sure doesn't look like a storm is coming." Bess looked up at the sky. The cloudless horizon was serene and blue as a robin's egg.

Josh smiled. "You won't see any actual storm clouds for a while, Bess. Right now the danger for swimmers is the killer riptides."

"A big offshore storm like this one creates a pressure system that acts like a giant suction cup, pulling water away from the beaches," Ruby explained.

Nancy was struck by a sudden thought. "George and Danny are still surfing back at the beach!" she exclaimed.

"That's right. Maybe the lifeguards there haven't heard about the riptide alert yet." Josh sounded worried.

"We'll have to look for the surfboard thief later

on," Nancy said. "Right now we'd better go warn the others about the riptides."

"Let's do it," Josh responded. They walked Ruby to the surf shop and hightailed it back to the beach in Josh's van.

"I don't see them anywhere," Nancy said. She, Josh, and Bess had arrived back at Honolua Beach to find Danny and George. The three of them stood near the Golf Coast tent, scanning the beach and the pier area for any sign of their friends.

The ocean's swell had increased several feet since they'd left only a few hours earlier. Above them, the sky was still clear and calm. The peaceful scene gave no clue that a dangerous undertow was building just beneath the surface of the water.

"Maybe they went to get a snack or something," Bess suggested.

"I hope you're right," Nancy replied.

When they arrived they had seen a lifeguard setting out a warning sign that read Danger—No Swimming. Another guard had been using a megaphone to order swimmers out of the water.

"I'll go tell one of the guards that we can't find our friends," Bess said.

"Good idea," Nancy said. "Josh and I'll check

our spot on the beach to see if Danny's surfing gear is still there."

"I'll catch up with you," Bess replied.

Nancy broke into a semi-trot as she and Josh made their way down the beach. She kept her eyes fastened on the sea until they reached the spot where they'd parked the cooler and chairs.

George's and Danny's surfboards were the only things missing, she noted with dismay. That meant they were probably still out on the ocean somewhere.

Nancy questioned a couple of young surfers who were lounging on their boards on the sand. The boys shook their heads when Nancy asked them if they'd seen anyone still surfing.

"Haven't seen anyone out there since they posted those No Swimming signs down the beach," one of them said. "We stayed in until a lifeguard chased us out. Bummer that we have to miss all this monster surf."

Nancy thanked them for the information.

Josh shook his head as he and Nancy walked away. "We call those real young surfers *groms*," he said to Nancy. "They're full of enthusiasm, but they've got a lot to learn about safe surfing."

They walked to the water's edge. Nancy held up a hand to block the glare of the late-afternoon sun as she scanned the horizon. At last she spotted two heads bobbing far out in the water and then caught a glimpse of George's red-striped surfboard.

"There they are!" Nancy exclaimed to Josh. After cupping her hands over her mouth to form a megaphone, she shouted, "George, Danny— come back in!"

She shouted a few times but soon lowered her hands. It was no use, she realized. They were much too far out. Even if she had used a bull-horn, she couldn't have been heard from that distance over the roar of the surf.

"I wonder if they realize how far out they've drifted." Josh sounded uneasy. "That's why rip-tides are so dangerous. The current pulls you out so slowly you don't realize you're in trouble until it's too late."

"Josh, can you go find Bess and the lifeguard?" Nancy said urgently. "Maybe they've got a res-cue boat. I'll stay here and keep an eye out so we don't lose sight of them."

"You got it," Josh called over his shoulder, already on the move.

While Josh headed back toward the pier, Nancy kept an anxious watch. She could see Danny catch a wave and begin to cruise toward shore. Soon George was standing on her board and steering right into the curl of a towering twenty-foot wave. You can do it, George, Nancy silently urged.

For a while things went smoothly. Then all of a sudden the solid wave appeared to break up because of a crosscurrent. The lip of the wave's curl collapsed, causing a two-story wall of water to come crashing down on top of George's head.

Nancy caught her breath as George's surfboard catapulted through the air. Where is she? Nancy thought anxiously. Then she spotted her. George had been thrown off the board and was in the water.

Her arms churned furiously as she fought her way through the waves back to the board, but it seemed to Nancy that her friend was starting to weaken. George's head disappeared under a whitecap.

When she reappeared, she was farther out in open sea. As Nancy watched helplessly, George was tossed high by one rolling wave, then crashed down with the next. Her head disappeared from view again.

Nancy felt an electric shock run through her body as she realized what was happening. Her best friend George would drown if Nancy didn't get help fast!

4

Too Close for Comfort

Nancy glanced around desperately for something to use to reach George. She knew she had to act quickly—time was running out.

She dashed back to the spot where the young surfer groms were lounging on their boards. "I need to use your board," she shouted to one boy.

"There's a riptide warning up," the startled boy replied.

"My friend's in trouble," Nancy stated simply, taking the board from the outstretched hands of the grom.

Nancy took a running leap into the surf to launch herself, not worrying about her own safety. She lay stomach-down on the board and paddled furiously with her arms, heading for the spot where George's head had disappeared. Her progress was slowed by the rise and fall of the ocean's swell.

Nancy scanned the area for George, but saw no sign of her friend. Then all at once she spotted her drifting far off to the left. Nancy couldn't tell if George was conscious. Had she arrived too late? Nancy wondered, fighting off a sense of panic.

At that moment Nancy's attention was drawn by a noise near shore. She turned her head in time to see a figure streak into the water from the pier. The man had on the bright orange swim trunks worn by lifeguards on that beach.

With an awesome display of strength and speed, the lifeguard's muscular arms sent up a spray of glistening water as he sliced his way through the waves toward George.

Nancy and the lifeguard reached George at almost the same moment. The lifeguard pulled out a brightly colored plastic square that automatically inflated to become an emergency float. He placed the float under George's shoulders.

"Now let's push her up onto your board," he instructed Nancy. Together, the lifeguard and Nancy pushed a limp George onto the surfboard.

Nancy assisted him with a numb sense of shock—it was hard to register what was happening to her friend. The lifeguard was gently turning George's head to clear her nasal passages of seawater.

Soon they heard the low, buzzing sound of a boat's engine approaching. "Here comes Rescue," the lifeguard said.

One of the lifeguards whom Nancy had seen on the beach earlier pulled alongside them in an emergency boat. She idled the engine and helped them pull George into the boat. The other lifeguard performed CPR while they raced back to shore.

Bess, Josh, and Danny stood in an anxious huddle along with a group of onlookers back at the beach. The lifeguard stretched George onto the sand and continued performing CPR.

Bess's face was ghostly pale. Her eyes were full of fear as she looked down at her cousin lying on the beach. "Nancy, is she breathing?" she said.

Nancy gave Bess a quick hug. Nancy's own heart was too full of worry at that moment to reply to the question.

"Come on George," she whispered urgently under her breath. "Hang in there. Don't give up on us."

After an agonizingly long minute, George flinched and coughed up a lungful of seawater. Her eyes slowly fluttered open, and she looked up at Nancy and Bess with a dazed expression.

"What's up?" she murmured.

"George," Nancy said with relief as she clutched her friend's hand.

"Thank goodness you're okay!" Bess cried. A cheer went up from the people who were looking on.

"You're going to be okay now, George," the lifeguard said. "We just need to get you to Emergency, where you can be checked by a doctor."

"Way to go, Manny," Josh said to the lifeguard. "This is our ace rescue guy, Manny Monolo," he said to Nancy and Bess.

"I'm no ace compared to you—right, Josh?" Manny rebuffed Josh's praise as he briskly attended to George. "I guess that's because some of us get messed up by other people's mistakes," he continued. His tone sounded bitter, Nancy noticed.

Josh shrugged and shook his head. "Whatever you say, Manny," he said, glancing away.

Nancy briefly wondered what was behind the lifeguard's bitterness. She would have to ask Josh about it, but later. Right now her main concern was George.

"Are you comfortable enough?" Danny's mother, Terra Takemura, handed George a cup of steaming herbal tea. George was propped up by numerous pillows and cushions in the guest bedroom of Danny's house. Nancy sat next to her in a chair.

"I'm fine, thanks, Mrs. Takemura." George smiled as she took a sip of the hot drink.

"Good to have you back in the world again." Nancy smiled warmly at her friend.

"The emergency room doctor said George is going to be fine. She just needs lots of rest and liquids," Danny's mother told Nancy. "I'll be mixing in a generous portion of that island hospitality we call aloha spirit," she added.

"There's nothing better for you than my island green tea," she said to George.

"I'm so grateful to everyone," George said as she took a sip of the fragrant tea.

"I'll be back to check on you in a little while, George," Nancy promised as she stepped outside the room. Josh, Bess, and Danny were waiting in the hallway.

"How is she?" Josh asked.

"She's okay," Nancy replied. "Talk about a narrow escape."

"If it hadn't been for you and Manny Monolo . . ." Danny shook his head as if to banish the thought. "Let's go out on the deck," he said. "I think I could use some of Mom's green tea."

Nancy breathed in the fragrant night air as she, Bess, Danny, and Josh stepped onto the front deck overlooking the Pacific. Sunset had turned the sky into a pearly dome of pink and purple clouds, and the evening's tropical breeze carried the faint scent of jasmine.

Nancy turned to Josh. "Speaking of Manny," she said, "what was going on between you two today back at the beach? He sounded angry with you for some reason."

"Yeah, I guess he is kind of sore at me," Josh replied. "I know it sounds odd, but I think he blames me for ruining his chances at a career."

"*His* career? You mean as a lifeguard?" Nancy asked.

"No." Josh shook his head. "All his life, Manny has wanted to be a paramedic," he explained to Nancy and Bess. "And he's perfect for a job like that. You saw him today—he's strong and skilled at saving lives."

"You're right," Bess said. "Being a paramedic sounds just right for a guy like Manny. So what's the problem?"

Josh hesitated. "Manny just can't control his temper. Last summer, he and I did an internship with the Emergency Medical Training School. I managed to goof up one of our exercises, and Manny really blew his top. He went so overboard that the instructor kicked him out of the program."

"And he blames you for getting him kicked out?" Nancy asked him.

Josh nodded. "Yes," he replied. "I was hoping it had all blown over, but today he was sounding like he's still holding a grudge. It's too bad. We used to be really great friends."

"Isn't it kind of immature for Manny to blame you for his own bad behavior?" Bess asked.

Josh and Danny glanced at each other.

"Bess is right on that one, Josh," Danny replied with a half-grin. "But then, no one has ever accused Manny of being mature. It's something he's going to have to work out for himself."

Josh stood up and stretched. "It's been a long day," he said. "Let's all get together tomorrow, shall we?" he said.

"Good idea," Danny said. "We'll come by in the morning and pick you up in my Jeep. We'll have brunch in town and then see what we want to do."

"Sounds perfect. Just one more thing," Josh said. He reached past Danny and plucked two scarlet hibiscus flowers from a blooming shrub. "For you," he said, offering the flowers to Bess and Nancy.

Bess blushed and tucked the flower behind her ear.

"Thank you," Nancy said. "And thanks for everything else. See you tomorrow."

*　*　*

The next morning was Thursday, and Nancy was up with the sun. Noting that Bess was still asleep, Nancy tiptoed around, grabbed a robe, and silently stole outside to catch a view of the sunrise.

She stepped onto the porch and looked out across the Pacific Ocean. Dawn had broken to reveal a flat, windless calm. There was no sign of the killer surf from the day before, she noticed.

"They call this the calm before the storm," Danny said, appearing behind her. "You'd never know by looking out there that a big blow is coming our way."

"We won't be doing any surfing today, that's for sure," Nancy said, looking at the smooth, glassy water.

Danny nodded. "Hey, I know what we can do after brunch! How about some snorkeling? I know a great spot—Shipwreck Reef. There's an old sunken ship down there where you can see lots of great fish and marine life."

Before leaving for town, Nancy and Bess carried a tray in to George.

"Try this egg dish, George," Bess urged. "It smells really good."

"I'm sorry I'm going to miss your snorkeling trip. It sounds like fun," George said, taking a forkful of food.

"Dr. Tyler said you shouldn't get up until tomorrow," Nancy replied.

George sighed. "I know, but you know how hard it is for me to stay in bed all day," she complained.

"Hey, cousin, you're sounding cranky. That means you must be feeling better." Bess grinned.

"I guess you're right," George said with a laugh. "Good thing Danny's got this great collection of sports mags," she said, pointing to a stack by the bed. "I'll catch up on my reading while you're gone."

Danny was standing near the front door next to a pile of snorkeling gear. "Let's pick up Josh, then we'll head for Ruby's to rent some more masks and snorkels," he said.

Nancy, Bess, and Danny headed outside and around the house to Danny's white Jeep, which was parked in the driveway. As she approached, Nancy spotted a white envelope that had been shoved under the windshield wiper.

"Looks like somebody left you a note," she said to Danny.

"Josh could have left it last night," Danny replied. "Maybe he forgot to tell us something and didn't want to disturb us, since it was kind of late."

As Danny opened the note, tiny pieces of

colored paper fell out of the envelope and onto the ground.

Danny scanned the piece of paper, his face tense. "You'd better look at this, Nancy," he said, handing her the note.

Nancy smoothed open the piece of paper. The message inside was scrawled in heavy red marker. She read the note out loud. " 'If you're Josh's friend, tell him to stay away from the Golf Coast Surf-Off. If he competes, Josh Brightman is a dead man!' "

5

Wipeout!

"This has got to be some kind of stupid prank, Nancy." Danny's voice rose in anger.

Bess had picked up the pieces of paper that had fallen to the ground. "It's a photo of Josh surfing—and it's been slashed to pieces," she said with fear in her voice.

Nancy shook her head. "I'm afraid this is no prank, Danny," she said, looking at the note again. "This threat against Josh makes one thing clear. Yesterday's attempt to steal his surfboard could have been part of a plot to keep Josh out of the surfing contest. Maybe someone else wants the prize money for himself—or maybe there's another reason altogether."

She folded the paper back up and reached for

the door handle to the Jeep. "Let's go pick up Josh."

A short while later they arrived at Josh's apartment. The welcoming smile faded from his face when they showed him the threatening message. He followed them back to the car.

"Some crackpot must have sent this thing." He shrugged, tossing the note onto the hood of the Jeep.

Josh was acting unconcerned, but Nancy could tell that he was worried. "We were hoping you could help us identify the person who wrote this note," Nancy told him. "Do you recognize the handwriting?"

Josh picked up the paper and looked closely at the message. "No, this handwriting isn't familiar," he said at last. He raised his eyes suddenly. "Do you think it could be the guy who ran off with my board yesterday—that Snake guy?" he asked Nancy.

Nancy nodded. "That thought did cross my mind. But then, who else would be involved? Snake couldn't have been working alone. There has to be someone else who wants to scare you away from the surfing contest."

"Or worse," Bess said apprehensively. "Remember, the note said you'd be a dead man." Bess gave Josh a worried look. "Maybe you should consider not competing."

43

"No way." Josh shook his head. "I'm not going to let some joker run me off the biggest surfing contest of the year," he stated flatly.

"I agree with you, Josh," Nancy said. "Let's go ahead with our plans for brunch and snorkeling today," she continued. "But let's all be super cautious."

Their first stop was Ruby's Place, where they shopped for some snorkeling gear and an underwater video camera. The shop was crowded with surfers who were picking up last-minute supplies for Saturday's Golf Coast Surf-Off.

"Hi, you guys." Ruby Blackwell looked up from some customers she was helping. "Back for more surfing? It's not much of a day for it, I'm afraid."

"We're going snorkeling after brunch today, out near Shipwreck Reef," Danny replied. "I want to show Nancy and Bess some of our underwater scenery."

"Ruby, you have a call on line one," a harried-looking clerk called out. The clerk was cradling a phone between his shoulder and ear as he waited on a customer at the front counter.

"I'll take it in the office, Neal," Ruby replied. "What a day!" she exclaimed to Nancy and the others. "Neal and I have been working here all night, doing our half-year inventory—just to keep the computer honest."

Ruby headed for the back of the shop and ducked through a doorway that was covered by a curtain of brightly colored beads.

A few minutes later Nancy was looking at a display of wetsuits near the doorway to Ruby's office, when she overheard Ruby talking on the phone.

"You know I'm good for it." Ruby's tone was low and tense. "I'll have the money for you next week, for sure." There was a long pause. "No, don't do that. Don't! You let me take care of it," she said.

Nancy thought she heard the telephone receiver being slammed down. She took a step back. Was Ruby in trouble? She had sounded afraid of the person she had been talking to on the phone.

Nancy pretended to be absorbed in looking at the wetsuits when Ruby brushed back the curtain of beads and came out, almost knocking into her.

"Nancy," Ruby said. "I didn't know you were standing right here. Is there anything I can show you?" Nancy thought that Ruby was startled and annoyed to see Nancy there.

"I was just looking around," Nancy replied. "I'll let you know if I need any help, though."

Ruby nodded and then made her way back to the customers she had been helping.

Nancy waited until Ruby and the clerk were

busy with customers up front. Then she tiptoed into the back office, taking care not to rattle the beaded curtain as she passed through it.

Nancy glanced around the small office. A collection of photos hanging on the wall were of Ruby surfing or posing with her board on different tropical beaches. The photos must date back to her professional surfing days, Nancy guessed.

On the desk Nancy noticed a stack of envelopes stuck on a spindle. The envelope on top of the stack was stamped "Overdue Bill—Third Notice."

It looks like Ruby is in some kind of financial bind, Nancy thought to herself.

Ruby's phone conversation echoed uncomfortably in Nancy's mind. It sounded from the conversation as if Ruby were being blackmailed.

Just then Nancy heard someone step just outside the office. She peeked out and was relieved to see it was only a customer browsing. She slipped back outside through the beads, grateful that she hadn't been caught snooping.

Nancy returned to join her friends up front. "I guess we've got everything," Danny announced. "Let's go grab some food."

On the way out they nearly bumped into Hank Carter, who was walking in the door. Hank was holding Ruby's sleek new Stinger surfboard under one arm. He stopped dead in his tracks when he spotted Josh.

"Hey, Josh, I took the Stinger for a trial run yesterday," Hank said. "And let me tell you, come Saturday this baby's going to run circles around you and your battered old board," he said.

"Lighten up, Hank," Josh replied easily. "This is a surfing contest, not a war."

Hank snorted. "These contests are battles, Josh," he replied. "If you don't know that by now, you might as well drop out. You'll never make the big time." He brushed past them.

Josh shook his head. "Hank goes way over the top during these competitions," he said as they walked along the sidewalk. "Out on the waves he's cool as can be, but with people he's a total jerk."

Hank seems angry at the world and totally obsessed with winning, Nancy thought. Was he driven enough to sabotage Josh, his main competitor?

Nancy turned to her friends. "You three go on and start eating," she said. "I want to ask Hank a few questions."

"Why—you think Hank could be involved?" Josh acted concerned. "He was out of bounds just now, but I've never thought of him as really dangerous."

"The threatening note this morning means that we have to examine everything—and everyone—in a new light," Nancy replied. "Hank's your main competition, and he's been trying to rattle you all week. I'd say he's the most obvious person to investigate."

Josh sighed. "Maybe you're right, Nancy," he said heavily.

Danny checked his watch. "Okay, Nancy. We'll meet you in an hour at a place called Papa's. It's about two blocks east," he said, waving to indicate the general direction of the restaurant.

After her friends left, Nancy hung around outside Ruby's Place until Hank reemerged. Hank acted surprised but pleased to see Nancy.

"Hey, how did you manage to lose your friends?" He smiled at her. "Well, that's good because I was hoping we'd have a chance to get to know each other."

Nancy forced herself to flash him a brilliant smile. "Hank, I'm trying to learn more about the surfing contest. Do you mind if I ask you a few questions?"

"Fire away," Hank replied. "I was just heading back to my place. You can tag along if you want."

Hank's friendly manner quickly faded as Nancy described the events of the morning, including her discovery of the note threatening

Josh. "We've been trying to figure this all out," Nancy said, looking him straight in the eye. "Do you have any ideas?"

"I haven't the faintest idea about all that." Hank's stare was piercing and stony. "And I certainly didn't have anything to do with it, if that's what you're getting at."

He shook his head. "I'd be an idiot to try something like threatening Josh—especially since I don't need to," he added, taking her by the elbow. "Come with me, Nancy. I want to show you something that might interest you."

Hank led Nancy around the corner and down a short block. They climbed a narrow flight of stairs to an airy apartment on the second floor.

Hank leaned his surfboard against the wall, walked across the room, and opened a cabinet that held a television set and VCR. "Now, watch this," he said, and pulled a videotape from the lower shelf of the cabinet.

Hank popped the tape into the VCR. The screen brightened with various shots that showed Hank performing daring maneuvers in various surfing contests. The video was underscored with music and professional-sounding narration.

"A television sports show in California taped this when I won the Sundown Surf Contest in Huntington Beach," he said with a note of pride.

On the tape, Hank demonstrated some truly

impressive surfing moves, including the difficult 360-degree air spin.

When the tape had finished, Hank turned to face Nancy. "You see, I don't need to scare Josh away from the contest this week—I'm going to win it fair and square," he said.

Hank rewound the tape and swung open the door of his video cabinet. As he replaced his tape into the display rack, Nancy spotted a video labeled "J.B." tucked way in the back of the cabinet.

J.B. might stand for Josh Brightman, Nancy thought. It might mean something very important. Nancy made a mental note to come back to check out the videotape when she got a chance.

Just then there was the loud sound of a door being banged open behind them. Before Nancy could turn around, the sound of a woman's shrill voice shattered the air.

"I've caught you, Hank Carter," the voice rasped close to Nancy's ear. The voice was then lowered to a menacing growl. "I know just what you're doing. And you can't deny it this time!"

Nancy turned. Standing behind them in the doorway was Marisa, Hank's girlfriend.

6

In the Red

"The minute I turn my back, you're chasing another girl," Marisa spat at Hank. "This is the last time, I'm telling you. I'm never seeing you again!"

"Come on, Marisa," Hank took a step toward his girlfriend. But Marisa was having none of it. She stormed around the apartment and picked up a jacket she had left there.

"Come on, nothing!" she yelled. "I know you're still hung up on Ruby Blackwell. You can never stop talking about her. And as if that's not enough, now I find you here with *her*," she added.

Hank glanced at Nancy and raised his hands in a helpless gesture. "Marisa is always getting these weird ideas about me and other girls," he said, shrugging his shoulders. "I don't know why."

Nancy had to suppress a smile at Hank's protest of innocence. From the interest he displayed in Nancy, she figured he gave Marisa a lot of reason to be jealous.

Hank followed a step behind his girlfriend as she strode angrily around the room. "Marisa, you're wrong about Ruby," he argued. "I'm not still hung up on her. Ruby and I called it quits two years ago."

"Hah!" Marisa wheeled about to face him. "Then explain to me why you lent her the last of your sponsorship money to fund that surfboard design of hers, that Stinger thing. You gave her that money last spring, and then you were too broke to do anything with me."

She broke into a stifled sob and stomped off into the bathroom.

"I'd better go—it looks like you two have a lot to deal with right now," Nancy said to Hank.

Hank said nothing and nodded glumly.

"One more question, Hank." Nancy paused at the door. "About that money you lent Ruby last spring—is she having some kind of financial problems?"

"No, there's no problem there," Hank responded quickly. "That is, none that I know of. I really have no idea. . . ." His voice trailed off unconvincingly, and he avoided meeting Nancy's gaze.

Nancy nodded briefly and said nothing further. She retreated down the apartment stairs, leaving the couple to their quarrel.

Nancy had the distinct feeling that Hank had evaded her question about Ruby's finances—or outright lied about them. She wondered if Marisa was right about Hank's still having a crush on Ruby.

Nancy glanced at her watch. It was ten minutes before noon. There was just enough time for her to swing back to Ruby's Place before meeting her friends at the restaurant. She hoped to dig around for more information about Hank and Ruby. If the surf shop owner was having money troubles, it was worth checking out. Ruby had accepted a loan from Hank, Nancy thought. There might even have been other loans. Also, Marisa voiced her suspicion that Hank was still carrying a torch for his old girlfriend.

That would give Hank two possible motives as a suspect in the campaign against Josh, Nancy figured. He wanted to help Ruby financially, and satisfy his own obsessive need to win the Golf Coast surfing contest.

At the surf shop, Ruby seemed surprised to see Nancy again. "Did you forget something when you were in here before?" she said.

Nancy shook her head. "Actually, Ruby, I'm trying to help Josh figure out what's been going on during the past two days. I wanted to ask you some questions."

Ruby's expression turned serious. "Let's talk in back," she said. "Neal, take over the counter for me," she called to the clerk as she led the way to the office in the back of the shop.

Ruby sat in a chair at her desk and pulled out a rag to wipe her hands. "I'm forever wiping this glittery wax off my fingers," she said. She raised her hand to show Nancy her sparkling fingertips. "We mix special pots of surfboard wax with iridescent glitter. It's a real popular item with the girl surfers."

Ruby tossed the rag aside and motioned Nancy to pull up a side chair. "Now tell me what's going on with Josh," Ruby said to Nancy.

Nancy told her about the note warning Josh to stay away from the Golf Coast Surf-Off. "The note threatened that Josh could be killed if he competes," Nancy explained. "We think the threat might be connected to the attempt yesterday to steal his surfboard."

"Wow, I can't believe it." Ruby leaned back in her chair with a shocked expression. "I was sure that that incident with someone attempting to steal the surfboard was just a fluke." She reached for a pencil-filled cup on the desk. "Any idea who might have left the note this morning?" she asked, fingering one of the pencils.

"Not yet," Nancy replied. "Right now I'm looking for anyone who might have a motive to keep Josh out of the contest."

"I don't understand." Ruby sounded confused. "What motive could there be?"

"Money, for one. Or revenge," Nancy suggested.

Ruby shook her head. "Josh doesn't have any real enemies that I know of, except maybe Russell—Captain Frye," she said slowly. "I heard that he's vowing to pay back Josh for having his shark operation shut down."

Nancy nodded. "Frye's definitely a possibility. But I was also wondering about a money angle."

"Money angle?" Ruby looked puzzled. "What do you mean?" she asked.

"Maybe somebody really needs that prize money right now," Nancy suggested.

Ruby threw back her head and laughed out loud. "In that case, I'm afraid you're talking about every single one of the surfers," she replied. "Even the most successful ones barely make ends meet from one contest to the next," she explained. "You don't see many surfing champions get paid to put their faces on a cereal box. At least no one rewarded me that way," she added.

A trace of bitterness had crept into Ruby's voice, Nancy noticed.

Nancy glanced at the array of trophies around the room and photographs that were hanging on the wall. "So, with all the surfing prizes and trophies that you won during your career, Ruby, you didn't come away with a lot of money?" she asked.

Ruby pointed to a gold trophy that was in a corner of the office. The trophy, which featured a woman riding a surfboard, was the largest Nancy had ever seen. It stood nearly two feet high.

"I won that trophy for first prize in the World Cup in the Antilles," Ruby said proudly. "I earned just enough money from that one to start Ruby's Place. But big prizes are few and far between, especially for female surfers. I kind of wish I were still on the circuit. Women are getting much more recognition and money these days." She sighed. "Anyway, I'm happy enough running my own business."

"So, business must be pretty good," Nancy said.

Ruby smiled. "So good, in fact, that I'm hoping to retire before I'm thirty—mainly on the strength of my new products," she said.

"I was just talking to Hank Carter," Nancy said.

"You were talking to Hank? What about?" Ruby's tone became guarded, Nancy noticed.

"Just stuff about surfing," Nancy said casually. She didn't want to let on the extent of her investigation—not yet, anyway. "He seems to have a lot of respect for you."

At that, Ruby's expression softened. She smiled. "You know, underneath that prickly exterior of his, Hank really is a great guy," she said gently.

Ruby gazed out the window as if she were looking into the past. "Hank and I went together for a couple of years. We were even planning to get married. But we were always separated so long during our surfing tours that we eventually drifted apart."

Ruby sighed and shook her head. "We both tried hard to stay together, but we could never get it back."

Nancy felt an unexpected surge of empathy for the young surf shop owner. "It's too bad how some things turn out, isn't it?" she said gently.

She checked her watch. "I've got to go. I'm running late for brunch with Josh and everyone," Nancy said. "Thanks for your time. And thanks for sharing so much about yourself," she added gently.

"No problem," Ruby replied. She glanced up at Nancy with a faraway expression in her eyes. She seemed to be thinking about Hank and what her life might have been with him.

Nancy said goodbye, then made her way to the front of the store and hurried down the street to meet her friends. Papa's was a cute restaurant that had a line of people out the door waiting to be seated. It was obviously popular for brunch.

Nancy made her way inside and looked around the restaurant for her friends.

"There she is." Bess's voice greeted her from a corner table.

"Sorry I'm late," Nancy said, slipping into a chair next to Danny. She gazed around the restaurant and then out the window overlooking the street. "What a pretty spot," she said.

A waitress placed a steaming plate of eggs and macadamia nut waffles in front of her.

"We went ahead and ordered the house specialty for you," Danny said with a grin. "I hope you're hungry."

Bess glanced from Nancy's plate to her own, which featured some dry toast and a fruit salad. "Maybe I'll have a bite of yours." Bess reached over and speared a piece of Nancy's waffle with her fork. "And just a little syrup to go with it," she added, pouring maple syrup on top.

"You were gone so long, we thought maybe Hank had kidnapped you," Danny joked.

"No such luck for him." Nancy grinned. "In fact, I think that Hank . . ."

Nancy's words trailed off as she noticed someone passing by the window. Suddenly she sat bolt upright.

"What is it, Nancy?" Josh asked. He swiveled around in his chair. Nancy had already jumped to her feet.

"Look, Josh," she said, pointing out the window. "It's the Snake—the guy who grabbed your surfboard yesterday!"

7

Another Close Call

The people waiting in line for a table gaped at Nancy as she rushed past them, hard on the heels of the Snake.

The Snake turned left onto the main street, which sloped gently downhill toward the harbor and the marina. Then he disappeared from view.

Not this time, you don't, Nancy thought. Dodging around a slow-moving truck, she kept pace with the Snake. He rushed down to a small courtyard shopping plaza that was fronted by half a dozen stores. Breaking into a run, Nancy arrived at the courtyard just seconds after the Snake.

The courtyard was filled with shoppers and tourists who had gotten off two double-decker tour buses parked in a nearby alley. Nancy heard a burst of tinny music, followed by scattered laughter and applause from the surrounding crowd.

Nancy glanced left and right. The tourists around her were watching the antics of a street musician and his companion, a black and white monkey. The musician fingered an old-fashioned accordion while the long-tailed monkey performed tricks, to the delight of the onlookers.

Nancy edged her way through the crowd, searching for several minutes for any sign of the Snake. Finally she spotted him. He was making his way down the alley past the buses.

Nancy resumed her pursuit down the narrow alleyway, which was dotted with garbage cans. Some of the cans were empty, Nancy noticed. They had fallen over and were lying out in the open. Dodging the cans, Nancy came within a few feet of the Snake.

"Hey," she called. "I just need to talk to you."

The Snake wheeled around, and for one moment he locked eyes with Nancy. Nancy felt a chill run through her. The expression in his dark eyes reflected the wild look of an animal about to be trapped.

In one swift maneuver, the Snake leaped over a fallen garbage can and kicked it back at Nancy. She tripped over the can and fell toward the pavement. She felt a stinging pain in her right knee as she went down. She was close enough to the Snake, though, to make one final attempt to catch him. She lunged forward and managed to grab hold of his jacket.

The Snake shrugged out of his jacket and fled, leaving Nancy holding it.

As she got to her feet, she could see that the Snake had reached the end of the alley. Just then a garbage truck lumbered by. The Snake grabbed one of the outside handholds on the truck and, clinging to the side of the truck, made his escape. Nancy stood helpless as she watched the truck disappear from view.

"Nancy!" Josh cried from the entrance to the alley. He ran toward her, with Bess and Danny close behind him. "We thought we'd lost you again. Are you okay?" he asked, looking down at her dirt-smeared leg.

"Just banged up a little," Nancy said, dismissing her discomfort. She described her pursuit of the Snake and his escape on the garbage truck. "But I managed to grab his windbreaker," she said. She began to search through the pockets. "Maybe there's a clue in here."

The pockets were empty except for a single scrap of shiny paper. One side of the paper had a number written on it and the words *Cutter One.*

"'Cutter One,'" Nancy read. "I wonder what this means."

"It could be a code," Josh said.

"It could be the name of a place," Danny said.

"Or a boat," Bess suggested.

"Or a telephone number," Nancy said thoughtfully. "If you spell out the word *Cutter* and then use a numeral in place of the word *one*, that would give us seven digits—the length of a phone number. Let's try it," she said.

They returned to the plaza and found a pay phone. After depositing a coin, Nancy pressed the numbers that corresponded to C-U-T-T-E-R-1. Nothing happened.

Then she tried the number that was written on the piece of paper. A phone rang. After a few rings Nancy could hear the line being picked up. "The mobile marine customer you have dialed is not available. Try again later," a recorded message announced.

"Marine customer," Nancy said, hanging up the phone. "Maybe Cutter One is the name of the boat with that number. We can try again after we go snorkeling."

"Good idea," Danny said enthusiastically. "Let's take a break and enjoy the rest of the day. We'll take the *Wind Song*. It's my parents' boat. Dad said we could have her all day."

The group returned to Danny's Jeep and piled

in. The snorkeling gear they'd rented was loaded in back.

"You guys are going to love Shipwreck Reef," Josh told Nancy and Bess. "I've never seen such a huge variety of marine life in one spot."

"We won't see any sharks, I hope," Bess said lightly, but her tone was only half-joking.

Danny shook his head. "Sharks are out there for sure, Bess, but most of them aren't dangerous to people. And even the big meat eaters naturally want to leave us alone," he explained.

"That's why what Frye is doing with his shark tourist attraction is so rotten," Josh said. "By luring sharks in with chum bait and feeding them, he's altering their natural behavior and making them much more dangerous to people."

"I can't understand why anyone would even want to watch a shark eat that bait you were describing to us yesterday," Bess said. "It sounds disgusting."

Josh shrugged, "People are funny that way," he said. "I think it's the same kind of curiosity that makes people slow down when they see a traffic accident."

On the drive back to Danny's house to get to his parents' boat, Nancy told everyone about her visit to Hank's apartment, Marisa's outburst, and her conversation with Ruby.

64

"I noticed that Hank has a videotape marked with your initials," she said to Josh. "At some point I want to go back there and take a look at that tape."

"I can help you do that," Josh replied. "I know where Hank keeps the spare key to his apartment."

"You said you were questioning Ruby, too," Bess said to Nancy. "Why? Do you think it's possible she's involved in all this?"

"Yes," Nancy said. "She said that the store was doing well, but I saw a stack of overdue bills. Plus, she's borrowed money from Hank to promote her new surfboard, the Stinger."

She described Marisa's suspicion that Hank still had feelings for his ex-girlfriend. "It's conceivable that Hank could be trying to make sure he wins the contest in order to help Ruby financially. Or maybe he's just driven by his own obsessive need to win the contest at any cost."

"There's no way that Ruby could be involved in anything underhanded, with or without Hank." Danny said firmly. "The whole town loves her—she's the closest thing we have to royalty around here."

"But you're right about one thing, Nancy," Josh added. "Surf shops in general are usually poor investments. Folks like Ruby get into the business out of their love for the sport. It's a way for her to stay involved with the sport even after she's stopped competing. But she'd be lucky to clear even a small profit. Most surf shops I've known close within five years."

Danny flicked a finger against a miniature surfboard that was dangling from his rearview mirror. "Yeah, the only way to make any real money in the surfing business is to come up with a great new surfboard design. She could either market it to other stores or sell the design to one of the big manufacturers."

"A new surfboard design—you mean like the Stinger?" Nancy asked.

Josh nodded. "Yes. That's probably why Ruby is pushing it so hard to everyone competing in the Golf Coast this week. She's hoping to get exposure for the product. But most of the competitors are like me—they've already got their favorite boards. I think Hank is the only one who's agreed to ride the Stinger in the contest."

Before boarding the *Wind Song*, Nancy and Bess headed for Danny's house to see how George was doing. Mrs. Takemura met them in the hallway just outside George's bedroom door. She raised a finger to her lips. "George has been sleeping for two hours," she whispered to Nancy. "The poor dear wouldn't admit it, but I think she really needed the rest."

"Please tell her we came in to see how she was doing, Mrs. Takemura," Nancy said. "We'll come right back after we finish snorkeling."

"Have fun out there." Mrs. Takemura smiled at them. "Just be sure not to wear any bright-colored jewelry," she said, glancing at Bess's sparkling pink ring.

"Why?" Bess asked, looking down at her ring with a nervous expression.

"Anything that sparkles attracts barracudas. . . ." Mrs. Takemura's voice trailed off as she disappeared back down the hallway toward the kitchen.

Nancy followed Bess into the living room.

"Barracudas, sharks—I'm not too sure about this whole snorkeling thing, Nancy," Bess said as she took off her ring. "What about these earrings?" She peered anxiously into a mirror on the wall. "Do they look shiny to you?"

"No, they're dark, Bess," Nancy said reassuringly.

"Still, you can't be too sure." Bess took off her earrings as well. She pulled back her lips to show her teeth. "Are my teeth sparkling?"

"Chill out, Bess!" Nancy laughed as she linked arms with her friend. "You'll be all right, I promise," she said. "As long as you take your seasick pill!"

* * *

67

About an hour later they dropped anchor at Shipwreck Reef. Maui lay to the east. To the west, a handful of tiny islands formed a dotted line to the horizon.

"The water gets shallow at the edges of this channel," Danny explained. "That's why so many ships went down here before they drew up decent naval charts."

"Bad luck for mariners but great for snorkeling," Josh added. "The fish love to hang around old sunken ships. To them it's just like a reef."

After strapping on masks, fins, and snorkels, the group plunged off the boat's swim platform and looked through their masks into a totally different world. Shafts of golden sunlight probed the aquamarine depths beneath them as the four snorkelers made their way forward.

Under its placid blue surface, the ocean was teeming with life. The fish displayed no fear of the humans in their midst. Josh handed out bags of cut-up minnow so they could feed some of the creatures by hand. Even Bess overcame her nervousness and allowed a big grouper with a sour-looking expression to take food from her.

About half an hour later Nancy heard a muffled roar from under the water. It sounded like a boat approaching. She swam to the surface and spotted a small motorboat not more than ten yards away. Nancy cleared her mask to get a better look. She couldn't believe her eyes.

Sitting hunched over in the boat was the Snake. He was holding a large plastic bucket in his hands. As Nancy watched, he dumped a red-colored substance from the bucket over the side of the boat and into the water. A large crimson stain spread out from the spot where he had poured out the bucket.

Nancy knew exactly what the Snake was doing. Her stomach contracted in fear. The red staining the water was chum bait, and dumping chum was a surefire way to attract sharks!

Quickly Nancy signaled to the others to return to the *Wind Song*. Her friends appeared to be confused, but they followed Nancy's direction. The four of them swam until they were within yards of the boat.

Nancy glanced over her shoulder for any sign of trouble. Too late, she spotted a squadron of shadowy sea creatures with triangular dorsal fins. The fins were slicing toward them through the waves, closing in fast.

Nancy's heart nearly stopped beating. Sharks! she thought in a panic. How will we get out of this one alive?

8

A Frightening Moment

"Hurry!" Nancy shouted to the others. She could see Bess tread water for a moment, then glance behind her. Nancy was sure Bess saw the pointy fins slicing through the water toward the group. The fins were about twenty yards away and moving in quickly.

Bess let out a small scream before she stopped treading water. Her head disappeared beneath the surface.

It was clear to Nancy that her friend was paralyzed with fear. "Help me get Bess up on the swim platform. She's panicking," she said to the others, and dove under for Bess.

Josh clambered up onto the narrow platform and leaned forward to grab Bess while Nancy guided her friend toward him. He held out a hand to her. "Come on, Bess. You can do it," he said.

Josh's gentle voice seemed to snap Bess out of her deep freeze. The scream that had stuck in her throat came out full-force now.

"Sharks!" she cried, pointing behind Nancy and Danny, who were still in the water.

The leading fin was almost upon them now. Nancy and Danny grabbed the rung holds along the side of the boat and quickly hoisted themselves up and onto the swim platform.

Nancy's foot had barely cleared the platform when the gleaming fin submerged directly underneath the boat. Bess and Danny reached out to help Nancy climb up onto the aft deck.

There was a moment of dead silence, broken by Bess's whisper. "Are they going to attack the boat, like in that shark movie?" she asked nervously.

Then something unexpected happened. The fin that had passed under the boat broke the surface on the other side. A large creature rose up from the water, then vaulted high into the air with a joyful leap.

"That wasn't a shark. It's a dolphin!" Nancy cried out.

"A dolphin—thank goodness. I love dolphins!" Bess collapsed into relieved laughter. She flung out her arms and somehow managed to hug Josh, Nancy, and Danny all at the same time.

The first dolphin was soon joined by two others. The three friendly mammals put on a great show of jumps, flips, and turns for the humans watching from the boat.

"I should have known those fins belonged to dolphins, not sharks," Josh chided himself. "I didn't stop to take a good look at them."

"If they had been sharks, you wouldn't have had time to stop and look," Nancy pointed out.

"You said it, Nancy." Danny laughed. "We'd all have been shark stew, for sure."

"Ugh!" Bess said. "Add stew to the list of things that are off my menu forever," she added miserably.

The playful dolphins arced back and forth over the wake of the *Wind Song* while Danny navigated back to Maui. His expression grew somber as Nancy told the group about seeing the Snake filling the water with chum bait. "We're lucky there were no sharks in the vicinity. When I think of what could have happened out there . . ." he said slowly.

Nancy nodded. "This incident was much more serious than the surfboard heist or that threatening note. The Snake could have killed us with that stunt out there today," she said.

"You didn't see any sign of Frye with him, did you?" Josh asked her.

Nancy shook her head. "The Snake was the only person in the boat. But from what you've said, the shark chumming is just the kind of business that Captain Frye is all about."

"Let's go back and confront Frye about this or report him to the police," Josh suggested.

Nancy shook her head. "We can't yet. We still don't have any real evidence against Frye. And remember how far we got with direct confrontation yesterday," she said, reminding them of Josh's near-violent episode with Frye. "We have to do some more investigating."

Nancy looked at Danny. "I'd like to do a background check on the Snake—see if we can find out who this guy really is. Danny, do you know anyone in local law enforcement?"

Danny thought for a second, then his expression brightened. "Hey, I know—Sergeant Danko. He recently retired from the Lahaina P.D. The sarge and my grandfather are great fishing buddies."

"I'd like to talk to him if he's around," Nancy said.

They dropped anchor at a small public beach near Sergeant Danko's house. After calling ahead to make sure he was home, they walked a pleas-

73

ant quarter mile on foot along an interior road to the officer's duplex apartment.

"Danny! And Josh Brightman—haven't seen *you* around for a while. How's the surf? Not too good today, looks like." Sergeant Danko shook Danny's and Josh's hands.

Danny introduced Nancy and Bess, and explained the reason for the visit. "I'll let Nancy fill you in on what's been happening," he said.

Nancy related the attempted theft of Josh's surfboard, the threatening note, and the shark-chumming incident.

"The guy we're looking for has a shaved head with a twisted black snake tattoo running the length of his arm. We call him the Snake," she told Danko. "We think he could be working with someone else to scare Josh away from the Golf Coast contest this week. Do you know of anyone who fits that description?"

"Interesting." Sergeant Danko rubbed his chin thoughtfully. "A snake tattoo is something I would remember. It doesn't ring a bell, though."

"We have a notation on a piece of paper we found in his jacket pocket," Nancy said. " 'Cutter One.' We thought it might be a phone number. When we dialed the number, a recording announced that it was a marine line."

Danko made a note. "I'll get my buddies on the

force to trace the number to see if it's registered locally. Keep me posted if you turn up anything else on this guy. We may be able to use it later."

"We've also had a run-in with Captain Russell Frye, who operates that shark-chumming attraction in Lahaina," Nancy said.

The sergeant looked up. "Now, Frye I know from way back," he said. "That guy's got a rap sheet a mile long. In fact, he just finished serving two months jail time for aggravated assault. If your Snake's hooked up with the likes of Russell Frye, he's found himself plenty of bad company."

Danko looked from Nancy to Josh. "I'll put the word out for the local police to keep a lookout for that Snake guy. And give me a call right away if he or Frye tries anything else. We want to keep our hometown boy healthy for the contest this week," he said.

They thanked Sergeant Danko and returned to Danny's house on the *Wind Song*. George was sitting out on the front porch when they arrived home.

"Hey, you guys went off without me?" She grinned at them.

"It's not as much fun without you, George," Nancy replied. "How are you feeling?"

"Like a wild mustang penned up in a corral,"

George declared. "I feel terrific, but Danny's mom is enforcing Dr. Tyler's orders that I rest one more day."

Nancy told George about their latest run-in with the Snake, including the shark scare.

"That guy is bad news," George said. "Bess, you must have been scared stiff," she said to her cousin.

"As a matter of fact I was," Bess replied. "Remember that game we used to play as kids— freeze tag, I think we called it? That was me out there. I froze like a statue in the water and was about to sink to the bottom until Nan came to my rescue."

"She got melted out real quick, though," Josh said, grinning at Bess.

"So, what's next in the investigation?" George asked Nancy.

Nancy checked her watch. "I want to interview those two surfers who got injured before all this started happening to Josh. If there's any link among these events, I want to find it."

Danny emerged from the house, a portable phone in his hand. "I just called as you asked, Nancy. Jo Jo and Keiko are still staying at the same place—the Jasmine Sea Motel."

Nancy and her friends made a quick snack of sliced bread, cheese, and apples in Danny's kitchen. Then Nancy, Josh, Bess, and Danny took

76

the Jeep into town to the Jasmine Sea Motel. There they met Keiko Mann and Jo Jo Sergeant. The two surfers were sunbathing on the front lawn. Jo Jo had his leg propped up in a cast. Keiko was lounging in bright-colored cotton shorts and sandals.

"Hey, Josh. Welcome to the recovery ward." Keiko greeted his friend. The wiry surfer was still pale from a bad case of food poisoning he'd contracted a few days before. The illness was what forced him to withdraw from the Golf Coast contest, he told the group.

"Man, I thought I was going to die," Keiko told them, when Nancy asked how he'd gotten sick. "The docs said it must've been bad seafood or something."

"Did you notice anything strange or unusual before you came down with the food poisoning?" Nancy asked him.

Keiko shook his head. "I stuffed my face at a seafood banquet the night I got sick—but that's not too unusual for me," he said with a lopsided grin.

Nancy looked at Jo Jo's leg in a cast. "How about you? How did you get injured?"

Jo Jo shook his head ruefully. "Tripped over a stupid skateboard someone left right outside my door," he said. "Some kid must've left it there."

"And did anything out of the ordinary happen

right before or after your injury?" Nancy repeated her earlier question to Keiko.

Jo Jo thought back. "Nothing that I can think of."

"How about that fight you had with the lifeguard?" Keiko reminded Jo Jo. "Remember?"

Jo Jo grimaced. "Oh, yeah. I had a close encounter of the rude kind with that guy Manny Monolo. Come to think of it, he did threaten to send me to the hospital."

"Manny threatened you just before you were injured?" Nancy's voice rose with the question.

Jo Jo nodded. "Yeah, he got pretty steamed at me." Jo Jo explained what had happened. He had been surfing near some children when his surfboard went wild, knocking a youngster out cold. Manny had had to rescue the boy.

"The kid was okay, but then Manny shoves me and says he'll send me to the hospital if anything like that ever happens again," Jo Jo said. "I was feeling so lousy right then about hurting the kid that I didn't even get sore at Manny about the shoving."

"You can kind of understand Manny getting angry over a kid getting hurt," Danny observed.

Nancy nodded. "Yes, but Manny's threatening Jo Jo marks him as a possible suspect. And remember, Josh—on the day he rescued George, Manny made it clear he still holds a big grudge against you." She reminded Josh about Manny's lingering bitterness over losing the paramedic internship.

Josh sighed. "I just can't believe Manny would be behind the kind of mean stunts we've seen this week."

"Someone has it in for you, Josh-o, for sure," Danny said to his friend. "Let's just hope it isn't Manny.'"

Nancy and her friends went home for dinner that night. "I have to be up early tomorrow," Josh announced as he was leaving. "I'm surfing in an all-day showcase to kick off the Golf Coast competition."

Nancy looked at Josh. "I'd like to talk to someone at the school where you and Manny served as interns, Josh," she said. "Can you arrange it?"

"Sure thing," Josh replied. "I've been giving surfing lessons to one of the officers there. We've become buddies. I'll call tonight and arrange for you to visit."

The next morning Nancy and Bess borrowed the Jeep to visit the emergency medical training school where Josh and Manny had worked the previous summer. There they met Ian McPherson, the supervising instructor. Nancy told him she wanted to know more about Manny Monolo.

"Everything I'm about to tell you is off the record. I'm only meeting with you as a favor to Josh," McPherson told them flatly.

"And we appreciate it," Nancy said. "Josh told me how Manny got kicked out of the internship program last summer," she said.

McPherson shrugged. "Manny has the raw material to be a great paramedic or firefighter—whichever he chooses," he said. "But he's got to do some growing up first."

"It seems as if Manny blames Josh for what happened," Nancy commented.

The instructor shook his head. "Only Manny is to blame for what happened. Josh made a typical beginner's mistake on their training run, but Manny blew up like the world was ending. You can't have that kind of temper in a real emergency situation."

Ian paused. "Josh doesn't know this," the instructor added slowly, "but Manny threatened to 'burn Josh real bad,' as he put it, as payback for getting washed out. I never told Josh, because I thought Manny was just spouting off."

Nancy and Bess thanked the instructor for his time, and returned to the Jeep. "One thing is clear, Bess," Nancy observed on the ride back to Danny's house. "For such a nice guy, Josh has made a lot of enemies. First the mysterious Snake, then Frye, and now Manny Monolo."

"And don't forget about Mr. Hank 'Winning-Is-Everything' Carter," Bess replied. "I don't trust that arrogant super-jock one bit."

"I don't, either," Nancy responded. "In fact, I still need to check out that tape with Josh's name on it that Hank's got tucked away in his video cabinet."

As they climbed the steps to the front porch of Danny's house, Nancy and Bess saw Manny Monolo sitting on a deck chair next to George.

George smiled up at them. "My rescuer just stopped by to see how I was doing," she said. "Or maybe I should call him my knight in shining swimsuit," she added.

"Hello." Manny stood up and nodded at Nancy and Bess. "Well, I guess I'd better be leaving," he said to George.

"Wait a minute, Manny," Nancy said. "I want to ask you about something. What do you know about Keiko Mann and Jo Jo Sergeant having to drop out of the surfing competition? Do you know anything about threats against Josh?"

"Word's gotten around about Josh, and about Keiko and Jo Jo," Manny said slowly. "But I didn't think there was any connection. Is there?"

"Maybe," Nancy replied. "Say, for example, if the same person had been known to threaten any of them before the incidents occurred."

Manny's expression darkened. "I wouldn't

know anything about any threats against Jo Jo, Josh, *or* Keiko," he said stiffly. He turned to George. "Well, I'll see you on the beach," he said. With that, he brushed past Nancy, took the steps two at a time, and strode down the front path to the street.

"Manny was acting weird. It's like he thought you were accusing him of threatening Jo Jo and Josh," Bess said.

"Maybe I was," Nancy replied. "I just found out today that he did threaten Josh at one point."

George shook her head and looked at Nancy. "Nancy, even if Manny threatened Josh, I don't think he meant anything. I think he's got a really good heart."

"I hope you're right, George," Nancy said with a sigh.

A little later Josh arrived to join them for a special dinner. The Takemuras were preparing a traditional Hawaiian luau, or feast, to be held on the beach in front of their home.

"I've been looking forward to this all day," Josh said, setting down his small duffel bag on the front porch.

They all put aside the worries of recent incidents and concentrated on having fun. While Danny and his father roasted ham and fresh-caught tuna over a flaming pit dug in the sand, Mrs. Takemura put on the grass skirt she had kept over the years. She treated the three girls to a lesson in the slow, rhythmic moves of the traditional Hawaiian hula.

"Every one of the hulas tells an island story," she said, demonstrating the graceful arm movements.

"Wow, this is great exercise!" Bess exclaimed, swiveling her hips. "I wish they taught a hula class at my health club back home."

Next, Nancy, Bess, and George learned how to fashion beautiful leis out of pale orchids and hibiscus flowers.

For dinner they sat on the beach and enjoyed a meal of island vegetables and grilled ham and fish, followed by juicy pineapple sticks. They then passed around a big bowl of poi, a native island specialty. It consisted of taro root that had been pounded into a soft paste. They ate the poi in the traditional way, by dipping their fingers into the big bowl.

After dinner Nancy, Bess, George, and Mrs. Takemura hung their flower necklaces around the necks of Danny, Josh, and Mr. Takemura. Then they all danced late into the night on the lawn overlooking the Pacific.

A little later Nancy and Danny were sitting on the front porch, taking a break and watching the others dance.

"I've got to get some pictures of this," Josh

called from the lawn. "My camera's in my duffel bag."

He climbed the steps to the porch and unzipped his canvas bag. As Nancy watched him reach into the bag, she spotted something long and black moving inside.

"Josh, watch out!" she cried, leaping up from her chair. She tackled Josh headlong, knocking him to the floor.

"Oomph!" Josh had the air knocked out of him as he hit the deck. He raised up on one elbow, rubbing his jaw. "Hey, Nancy, what gives?" he exclaimed in a shocked tone.

"Look," Nancy cried out, pointing at Josh's duffel bag. A creature with glittering black eyes was poking its head out of the opening. Its mouth opened to reveal long fangs.

It was a deadly-looking snake!

9

One Attack Too Many

The reptile slithered out of Josh's bag and across the deck. "Whoa!" Josh scrambled back to get out of the snake's path.

Mr. Takemura came racing up the porch steps. "Danny, grab me that roasting stick and one of those extra trash bags!" he yelled to his son.

Danny quickly handed his father the requested objects. Mr. Takemura took the wooden stick and went after the snake. He caught it just as the snake was slithering down the porch steps. Mr. Takemura lifted the snake with the stick and grabbed it behind its neck. He dropped the reptile into the bag and quickly closed it.

"Terra, we'll need some of your pillow cases.

And call Animal Control. Tell them it's an emergency—a poisonous snake."

Mrs. Takemura hurried into the house. Josh handed Mr. Takemura a piece of cord from his bag, which he used to tie it closed.

"You were amazing the way you handled that snake, Mr. Takemura," Nancy said with admiration.

Danny's father grinned. "I caught more than my share of snakes when I served with the navy in the Pacific," he replied. "I guess you never forget how to do it."

Danny's mother returned with the pillow cases. Mr. Takemura carefully dropped the plastic bag with the snake into the cloth cases. "It's late, but Animal Control said they'd be right over," Danny's mother said.

"You said this was a poisonous snake," Nancy said to Mr. Takemura. "Are you sure?"

"Absolutely," he replied. "This snake had a wide head and long fangs, which means it must belong to the viper family. They're not native to Hawaii, which is why Animal Control is so quick to respond. Hawaii is so isolated that we have to protect our natural species from foreign animals that might wipe out the native population."

"Someone must have stuck that snake in your bag, Josh," Nancy said to him. "Did you leave it unattended today at any point?"

Josh's face was ashen. "I left the bag in my car for a while, and maybe in the locker room at the beach," he recalled.

"Did you see anyone hanging around those areas today?" Nancy asked.

"Not really—I bumped into Hank, of course, because we were both in the showcase. Manny Monolo was around, too."

When Animal Control arrived, the uniformed officer took the bag with the snake and carefully transferred it to a cage. He let out a long, low whistle. "This is a very dangerous snake—it's called a death adder," he said to the group. "They use those long fangs to inject a powerful poison that affects the nervous system. Strange, though," he concluded, "this type of snake is found only in Australia and a few other Pacific islands."

Nancy described how they'd discovered the snake in Josh's bag. "You're lucky to be alive, both of you," the officer said as he looked from Nancy to Josh.

The parting words of Ian McPherson suddenly echoed in Nancy's mind. Manny had said he'd burn Josh real bad some day as payback for getting washed out of the paramedic internship program. Could the snake attack have been Manny's way of making good on that promise of revenge? she wondered.

Josh hadn't said much throughout the entire incident with the snake. Nancy and Bess looked at him, then exchanged glances.

"What is it, Josh?" Bess asked gently.

"Someone planted that snake because of me," Josh said in a low voice. "First the note, then the shark chumming, and now this."

"It's not your fault, Josh," Bess said.

Josh's voice remained muffled. "Someone else besides me could have been hurt this week. I can't bear the idea of that happening because of me. Maybe I should drop out of the contest," he added, staring at the ground.

"No, Josh." Nancy spoke up. "We're getting closer to finding out who's behind all this. We'll never succeed if you drop out. You've got to compete tomorrow."

Josh paused to consider Nancy's words. "Okay, Nancy," he said finally. "I won't give up."

"All *right!*" Danny raised his arm and gave Josh a high-five. "I knew the Josh-man wouldn't let us down."

"Josh, you said you saw Hank and Manny Monolo at the beach today," Nancy said to Josh. "Was there any kind of tension between you and either of those two guys?"

Josh nodded. "Hank and I nearly got into a fight."

"A fight? What happened?" Bess asked.

"Hank sat right on my wave—and then he nearly bowled me over. Can you believe that?" he said, looking indignantly at Danny.

"What do you mean he was sitting on your wave?" Nancy asked.

"It's the number one dirty trick in surfing," Danny explained. "You sit right behind another surfer who's waiting for a wave. Then either you take the wave away from him, or you crowd him so much he can't get a good ride."

"I warned Hank I'd deck him if he tries that during the contest tomorrow," Josh told them.

"Hank will have to report to the contest early, same as you, right, Josh?" Nancy asked him.

"Yeah, sure," Josh replied. "Why?"

"I want to check out that videotape in his apartment," Nancy explained. "The one with your initials on it. Maybe it will give us some clue as to whether he's up to anything more serious than just sitting on your wave."

Josh leaned forward. "Hank keeps his spare key on a nail he stuck underneath a wooden chair on the entry deck," he said.

"Thank you," Nancy replied. "We'll stop off on our way to the contest tomorrow and watch a little TV."

* * *

89

The next day was Saturday, the day of the first heat of the Golf Coast contest. Nancy, Bess, George, and Danny rose early and grabbed a quick breakfast before driving to Lahaina.

"It feels so great to be out again," George declared with a big grin. "I was beginning to get seriously stir-crazy."

"We missed you a lot, George." Nancy gave her friend a warm smile.

When they arrived in Lahaina, Danny parked the Jeep along the street opposite Hank's apartment. They waited for a few minutes to make sure Hank wasn't still inside.

"His apartment looks empty," Danny observed. "Hank must have already left for the Golf Coast."

"Still, we should post a lookout, just in case he returns," Nancy said. "Bess, want to stand guard?"

"Sure," Bess replied. "I'll tap the horn three times if I see anyone."

Leaving Bess to keep watch, Nancy, George, and Danny climbed the steps to Hank's second-floor apartment. Nancy ran her hand along the bottom of a wooden deck chair to find the spare key. "Here it is," she announced, plucking the key off a tiny nail.

Nancy unlocked the door. Cautiously, they all

went inside. Nancy walked quickly across the living room and opened the cabinet that held the videotapes. She sorted through them until she found the one labeled J.B.

"Now we'll see what this is," she said. As she pulled the tape from its jacket, a folded piece of white paper fluttered to the ground. Nancy bent down to pick up the paper and read it.

"What does it say, Nancy?" George asked, peering over her shoulder.

"It looks like a list of some kind," Nancy replied. "Listen, it says 'One—use the dual cutback to offset J's inside curl; two—sit on his wave if J pulls ahead; three—'"

Nancy stopped reading. "Strange. That's all I can read. The rest of the list is blacked out with heavy marker."

"'Sit on his wave'! That means Hank is planning to win by playing dirty, just like he did yesterday," Danny said angrily. "I hope the judges don't let him get away with it."

"I wonder what was on the rest of this list," Nancy said. "I wonder if Hank had written down even nastier tactics he planned to use to rattle Josh."

"Like the slashed picture and note, or the planted snake," George said.

"Exactly, George," Nancy replied. She

popped the tape into the VCR. The tape was of Josh surfing during recent competitions.

"And look, Nancy—there are two other tapes marked Jo Jo and Keiko," George said, pointing to the back of the cabinet.

There were no lists tucked inside the tapes marked for Jo Jo and Keiko. "Maybe he threw their lists away," George suggested.

"What do you think, Nancy?" Danny asked when the tape ended.

"We have a list of dirty strategies Hank intends to use against Josh, plus this tape of Josh surfing," Nancy said as she rewound the tape. "We've also discovered tapes of the two surfers who came down sick or injured last week. At the very least I'd say Hank Carter has some explaining to do."

"What can we do about it?" George asked. "The contest is set to begin in a couple of hours."

"I'm going to confront Hank about this today, during the opening heat," Nancy declared. "At least it'll put him on notice that we're onto his unscrupulous tactics."

Danny glanced at his watch. "Speaking of the contest, we'd better get moving if we're going to make it on time."

They replaced the tapes and returned to the car. "I didn't see anyone the whole time," Bess said. "How'd it go in there?"

Nancy described what they'd found. Meanwhile, Danny pulled into a corner gas station a mile or so down the road to fill up. "Be right back—I'm going for a soda," Nancy announced.

"I'll come with you," Bess said as she opened her car door.

As they popped open their sodas, Nancy glanced down a row of shops across the street from the gas station. "Hey, look, Bess. There's Ruby Blackwell going into that shop," she said.

Ruby was entering a shop marked "Pawnshop—Trade Items for $$CASH$$."

"I wonder what she's doing in there," Bess said.

"Looks like she's giving something to the clerk," Nancy said. She narrowed her eyes to see better from the distance. "Let's stop a second. I want to see what she's doing exactly."

Ruby soon came out of the shop, hurried to her car, and got in without looking around. Then she started the engine and quickly drove off.

"Let's go check out the shop," Nancy said. She and Bess walked up to the pawnshop's display window. The counter clerk was setting a sparkling red ring into the display window.

Nancy peered closely at the ring. "I'm sure that belongs to Ruby," she said.

"She must need the money," Bess said.

"That's odd, because Ruby told me herself that her shop is having a great year financially. Let's go check it out," Nancy said.

"I was just noticing that red ring you have in the window," Nancy said to the young clerk behind the counter. "Can you tell me anything about it?"

"Well, we can't tell you where the stuff comes from," the clerk said, snapping her chewing gum. "But I can tell you that it's worth a lot. It's made out of real rubies. And it belonged to a real local celebrity. Ruby—oops, I shouldn't have told you the name." The girl clapped her hand over her mouth and giggled.

"I won't say a word," Nancy said with a smile. "I wonder why she sold it? The ring, I mean—it's so beautiful," she prompted the chatty clerk.

The girl leaned forward as if to share a big secret. "Well, you didn't hear this from me, but Ruby's been in here pawning a lot of stuff recently," she said. "I think she's kind of down on her luck, if you know what I mean," she added in a loud whisper.

"I know exactly what you mean," Nancy replied.

"What were you guys doing—drinking the whole soda truck?" George asked Nancy and Bess when they returned to the Jeep.

"I'll explain in a minute. Danny, can we make a quick stop at Ruby's Place?" Nancy asked.

"You got it," Danny said, starting the car.

Ruby was just leaving her shop when they arrived. "Hi there." Ruby looked surprised to see them. "I'm on my way to watch the Golf Coast," she told them.

"So are we," Nancy replied. They chatted for a second about the weather, which was getting windier by the hour from the tropical storm that was still hovering offshore. Then Nancy pretended to notice Ruby's missing navel ring. "Oh, Ruby, you're not wearing your pretty ring today!" she exclaimed.

Ruby looked uncomfortable. "Oh, I—I must've left it at home," she said.

Nancy decided to push further. "Funny how we keep seeing you today. We were just over getting some gas and saw you on the street outside one of the shops," she said.

Ruby avoided Nancy's gaze. "I think you must be mistaken. I've been here for the last couple of hours," she said.

Ruby looked at her watch. All of a sudden she seemed to be in a great hurry. "Well, I'm off now," she said. "See you guys at the Golf Coast."

"Well, that was an outright lie Ruby just told," Bess said to Nancy after Ruby was out of earshot.

95

"Yes, she certainly hasn't been here at the shop for the past two hours," Nancy said. "We know where she was—she was selling her ring. The question is, why?"

Nancy pressed her lips together thoughtfully. "And why did she lie to us just now?"

10

A Perfect Ten

"Maybe Ruby lied because she's embarrassed about needing money," George suggested.

"That's a good possibility," Nancy said. "But she made such a point of telling me her finances were in great shape the other day. She even said she hoped to retire soon. It was like she was expecting to get a lot of money in the near future."

"I don't know what Ruby's up to. But I do know we're going to be late for the contest if we don't leave right now," Danny said urgently.

"All right, Danny." Nancy grinned. "You win. My questions about Ruby can wait—for the moment. I'll try to catch up with her at the contest."

The first round of the Golf Coast Surf-Off was just getting under way when they arrived at Honolua Beach. The day was bright and balmy in spite of a steady wind and a layer of dark gray clouds that was building to the east.

A large crowd had turned out for the contest. Nancy and her friends joined a line of people streaming under a huge blue- and white-balloon banner that formed a floating archway over the entrance to the pier.

Next to the pier, surfers and spectators wandered in and out of the Golf Coast sponsor's tent. The aroma of buttered popcorn and roasted hot dogs mixed with the tropical fragrances in the air.

In the sky above them, an old-fashioned biplane pulled a long sign advertising Golf Coast sporting equipment.

"Josh said he reserved us some spots at the front of the viewing stands over there." Danny pointed to some wooden bleachers that had been placed along the main stretch of the beach.

From their vantage point on the pier, Nancy looked over the scene. She spotted Ruby Blackwell heading into the sponsor's tent. "You three go on and grab our seats," Nancy said. "I'm going to see if I can talk to Ruby for a second."

While Danny, Bess, and George headed for the bleachers, Nancy threaded her way through the crowds to the sponsor's tent. She wandered for a while among the sporting goods displays and food booths, but saw no sign of Ruby.

Nancy came upon a small trailer tucked away in a corner of the tent. "Private—Golf Coast VIP Welcome Office," she read on a gold-lettered sign posted on the side of the trailer.

A window of the trailer was slightly open, and Nancy heard voices coming from inside. One of the voices belonged to Ruby Blackwell.

"I don't care about the fine print—my contract included the full merchandising deal, including promotional costs!" Ruby was saying in a heated voice.

"Now, Ms. Blackwell," a man responded to her in words that sounded polite but firm. "The promotional clause kicks in on your contract only following a successful showing this week."

"We'll see about that," Ruby snapped. She flung open the door and steamed out of the trailer. Nancy quickly drew back and turned away so that Ruby wouldn't notice her standing there.

She tried to figure out the meaning of the conversation she'd just overheard. Ruby and the Golf Coast executive had been arguing over some kind of contract that Ruby had signed with the company. Could that deal involve the surfing contest? Nancy wondered. Why was Ruby so angry about it? Nancy knew she needed to find out.

Nancy waited for a few minutes. Sure enough, a man wearing a suit and a Golf Coast lapel pin soon left the trailer. Making sure she wasn't observed, Nancy ducked inside. She wanted to see if she could find any clue to the agreement Ruby had with Golf Coast.

Inside the cramped trailer, Nancy's glance took in the chairs and a table. The room was clean as a whistle—no paperwork and no other sign of anything to let Nancy know what kind of contract Ruby and the executive had been discussing.

Nancy felt annoyed with herself. Searching the booth had turned up nothing. She should have followed Ruby or the Golf Coast executive, she realized.

A voice over the loudspeaker announced the first heat of the Golf Coast Surf-Off, interrupting her thoughts.

"Next up, two respected locals—Josh Brightman, followed by Hank Carter," the announcer boomed.

Nancy headed back to the viewing stands. She'd have to follow up on Ruby's contract after Josh's first ride of the contest.

"Hey, Nancy." George handed her friend a

pair of binoculars when she arrived back at the bleachers. "Josh is over there."

"I'm stoked on this wave action today," Danny exclaimed. "That storm to the east is really making the surf go richer."

"That means you're excited because the storm is whipping up some monster waves for the contest—right?" Nancy grinned.

"You got it, Nan." Danny reached over and ruffled her strawberry blond hair.

Nancy peered through the binoculars at the competition area, which was roped off by bright orange-and-white buoys. She saw Josh floating far out, waiting for his first wave. When a powerful set of rollers moved in, Josh pushed himself forward with his arms. Rising up on the board, he took command of the lead wave as it built up into a majestic, towering curve.

"What a gnarly wave," Danny said. "Josh held back and waited for just the right one. Now you guys watch him pull out his bag of tricks."

Josh bore down on the curl, crouching low to reduce wind resistance and gather speed. Then he launched his board like a rocket into a spectacular 180-degree air spin and landed neatly back on the wave.

"Way to go, Josh-o! Now he'll shoot the curl," Danny said. "This is make-or-break time for his first ride," he told Nancy, Bess, and George. "He has to avoid being crushed if the curl collapses down on him."

Josh crouched down again as the lip of the wave curled over, forming a long, narrow tube. As they watched, Josh shot his board into the tube, disappearing from view. The tube appeared to close in over his head.

"Oh no . . ." Bess whispered. She grabbed the binoculars from Nancy and anxiously scanned the water for signs of Josh.

Next thing, the audience in the stands was bursting into applause. Josh had broken through the far end of the tube. His arms were raised triumphantly.

"Way to hot dog that wave, Josh!" Danny and George leaped up and cheered excitedly.

Bess turned to Nancy with shining eyes. "He makes it look so easy. That's what's so amazing."

There was a suspenseful pause as everyone waited for the judges to come up with their scores for Josh's performance. Then the judges raised their cards with the scores marked on them.

"Ten, nine-point-nine, ten, and ten!" Danny proclaimed. "Almost all perfect scores."

Now it was Hank's turn. He executed his ride with expert technical precision. But Hank's surfing style could not have been more different from Josh's. While Josh had cruised the waves with joyful ease, Hank appeared tense and studied.

When the judges posted Hank's scores for his first ride, the numbers were high, but they lagged behind Josh's. So far, Josh and Hank held the first two places in the standings.

"Josh is way in the lead," Danny said as soon as Hank's scores were announced. "They're scheduled for their next heat in an hour or so, so we can take a break. I'm going to go talk to some of my buddies down at the competition area."

"I'm hungry," Bess announced suddenly. "I could go for a hot dog right now."

"We'll go with you Bess," Nancy offered. "I'm in the mood for a dog with everything on it."

Bess, Nancy, and George headed out in search of their snacks. They bought three hot dogs from a man who was selling them from a box hanging on a strap around his neck.

As they ate, they talked about the case.

"Manny has a temper, I'm sure," George said, "but there's no way he staged all the stuff against Josh this week, like that note. It's got to be one of our other suspects."

"You're probably right," Nancy said to her friend.

They came across a crowd that had gathered outside the Golf Coast tent to watch a local reporter conducting an interview with Ruby

Blackwell. Ruby had her new surfboard, the Stinger, propped up next to her. She and the reporter were discussing recent advances in surfing and surfboard design.

"My new Stinger design represents an advance in the molding technique that offers less water drag. The result is greater speed," Ruby was saying. "We also use smaller fins that give the board cleaner, sharper turns."

"How's your new board doing in the contest today?" the reporter ask. "Isn't Hank Carter riding it?"

"Yes, Hank is doing quite well," Ruby replied with a big smile. "He's number two in the heats right now."

The reporter looked at the camera operator. "I think that's what we need," he said.

Nancy waited while Ruby and the reporter wrapped up the interview.

As Ruby was leaving the area, Nancy walked up and tapped her on the arm. "Hi, Ruby," she said. "Great interview. Was that the local sports anchor you were talking to?"

"Yeah." Ruby grinned. "I'm what passes for the local surfing expert around these parts."

"Are you working with Golf Coast? Is that why they asked you to do the interview just now?" Nancy asked her.

"Not at all." Ruby shook her head. "I did that

interview just now as a favor for the local reporter—and it was good promotion for my shop, I'll admit."

Nancy paused. Something didn't make sense to her. "So, you don't actually do business with Golf Coast? In terms of your shop, I mean," she pressed.

Ruby shrugged. "I've always got agreements going with the big sporting companies to sell their stuff," she said. "Golf Coast is just one of many product lines we sell at Ruby's Place."

She tapped Nancy lightly on the arm. "Hey, why all the questions? Am I on your list of suspects now?"

"Sorry, Ruby," Nancy replied. "I'm just trying to get the answer to some questions. And I want to get to know you better."

Ruby slipped an arm through Nancy's. "Well, that sounds good." She smiled. "Looks like everyone is having a great time. So, relax and enjoy the day, okay, Nancy?" she said.

Nancy watched as Ruby disappeared into the crowd. She realized she had begun to take a real liking to the surf shop owner. She hoped that Ruby was not involved in any of the attacks against Josh.

"What was that all about?" George asked as they returned to the bleachers.

Nancy described the conversation she'd overheard earlier between Ruby and the Golf Coast executive. "Ruby's got some kind of contract going with Golf Coast involving this contest, but she denied it just now," Nancy explained.

"That makes Ruby two for two in telling lies today," George said. "First about selling her ring, and now her contract. What gives?"

"I'm not sure," Nancy replied. "All I know is, something about that contract has got her pretty steamed up. I think the dispute had something to do with marketing and promotion. I just have a feeling it has something to do with the case, but I haven't figured out what yet."

They returned to the grandstands just as Josh and Hank were up for their final rides of the afternoon. Josh sat far out in the competition area, waiting for his wave.

When a set of huge waves rolled in, Josh caught one and rose up on the board, but something was clearly wrong this time. He staggered on the board and almost lost his balance. He missed the tube entirely.

Hank took his turn next. He performed well. His score for the ride was higher than Josh's, although Josh still clung to the overall lead.

Danny looked disappointed. "Josh lost it on that one," he said. "It's hard to see out that far, but it almost looked like Hank pushed him off his board."

The next surfer was just starting his ride when Nancy noticed a disturbance down on the area that was roped off for the contestants. Josh and Hank had squared off on the beach. Josh shook his fist angrily at Hank.

"It looks like trouble's brewing," Nancy said. "Let's get over there."

Nancy and Danny rushed down to the beach. By the time they arrived, some of the other surfers had pulled Josh and Hank apart. Marisa had already rushed to Hank's side.

Josh was breathing heavily. He glared at Hank. "Sit on my wave again and you're dead meat, Carter!" he snapped.

Hank looked unperturbed. "It was just an accident, Josh. The wave must have knocked me into you out there."

"While you're explaining things, Hank," Nancy spoke up. "Why don't you explain that tape you have at home? You know, the one that's marked with Josh's initials on it? I saw it that day we were in your apartment."

"That tape? Oh, that's nothing," Hank exclaimed angrily. "I keep tapes on all my competition."

"That might be true, but you deliberately sabotaged my ride," Josh said.

"Hey, you got a complaint, Brightman? Tell it to the judges." Hank turned away. Marisa gave

Nancy a triumphant look as she and Hank walked away, arm in arm.

"I'm okay. Let me go." Josh shook off the surfers' hands that had been restraining him. He stared after Hank and shook his head. "Forget it," he muttered. He looked at Bess and brightened.

"Hey, everybody's heading over to Big Waihine's for dinner. Let's go blow off some steam. The heats are over for today."

"Sounds great." Bess smiled.

A couple of hours later Nancy, Bess, George, Josh, and Danny were seated around a large table at Big Waihine's restaurant, which overlooked the fishing marina. They had an excellent dinner of grilled mahi-mahi and other local specialties.

"Mmm, I'm ready to burst." Nancy pushed back from the table. "I'm going for a quick walk around the boats."

Nancy had spotted Russell Frye's boat on the way in, and she wanted to check it out.

When Nancy walked down onto the docks, the *Shark Attack* looked buttoned up and deserted. She could see a couple of crew working late. It looked as if they were painting over the shark mural on the side of the ship. Maybe Frye was finally giving up on his chumming business, Nancy speculated.

There was no sign of Frye anywhere outside the ship, but Nancy could see a light shining inside.

The sun had just dipped over the horizon when Nancy returned to the restaurant. As she climbed the steps back to Big Waihine's, Bess rushed down the stairs toward her.

"Josh went to answer a phone call about fifteen minutes ago." Bess's voice was laced with anxiety. "And now we can't find him anywhere. He's disappeared!"

11

Snakebite

"Missing?" Nancy replied quickly. "Are you sure Josh didn't just go out for some air?"

Bess shook her head. "When he got the phone call, he said he'd be right back. That was ages ago. This restaurant isn't that big. We've looked all over the place for him."

Nancy followed Bess back to the restaurant's dining room. Danny and George met them at the table.

Danny's expression was tense. "I'm really starting to worry about Josh," he told Nancy. "This isn't like him at all. And with all those threats he's been getting . . ." His voiced trailed off.

"Who told Josh that he had a phone call?" Nancy asked.

"We all heard an announcement over the restaurant P.A. system," Danny replied.

"Let's start by talking to the restaurant staff," Nancy said. She headed in the direction of the kitchen.

None of the waiters or restaurant staff recalled announcing a phone call for Josh Brightman. Finally a young busboy spoke up. "There was a new waiter hanging around the kitchen near the intercom," he said hesitantly. "At least I thought he was a waiter. I remember him because I thought he looked kind of strange. But I'm new, so I didn't mention it."

"What did he look like?" Nancy asked the busboy.

"He had a shaved head, and when he turned around I saw he had a tattoo twisting all around his arm, like a black snake or something," the busboy replied.

The Snake! Nancy felt a sharp sense of dread in the pit of her stomach. If the Snake had anything to do with this, Josh could be in real trouble. Nancy turned to the others.

"Let's look around some more to see if we can turn up any signs of what happened," she said. "I'm going to search outside."

Nancy pushed open a side exit door and went outside. She walked down a pebbled walkway along the side of the restaurant, peering down at the ground as she went. A few yards from the door she caught a glimpse of something light colored that was crumpled up on the ground. She picked it up and shook out the pebbles.

"Look," she said to her friends as she rejoined them inside. She held up Josh's sky blue windbreaker. The jacket was torn, and there was a tiny streak of blood on it. It looked to Nancy as if the jacket had been ripped during a fight.

"Josh's jacket. Oh no." Danny sounded upset. "What do you think this means?"

"I think the Snake just made his move. He's kidnapped Josh." Nancy's reply was low and urgent. "We'd better call the police and make a missing persons report."

Bess's face got pale when they showed her Josh's jacket.

"What can we do? Nancy, I'm so afraid that something terrible has happened to him," she said, her voice cracking.

"The best thing we can do for Josh right now is to keep cool and think of everything we can do to find him," Nancy replied, putting an arm around Bess.

The police arrived a short time later, along with Sergeant Danko, whom Danny had called about Josh's disappearance. Danko reported to the uniformed officers about his earlier meeting with Danny and his friends.

The ranking officer looked up from the pad he was writing on. "Normally we wait a day or two when someone reports an adult person missing. Often they turn up on their own," he said. "But since we already have this report from Sergeant Danko, we'll start searching right away."

"Sergeant, were you able to track down any boat registered as *Cutter One*, the name that was on the note we found in the Snake's jacket?" Nancy asked Danko.

Danko shook his head. "Unfortunately, no. There's no vessel registered anywhere in Hawaii under that name. I even checked California listings. Nothing turned up there, either."

He looked around at the disappointed faces. "Don't worry. We're going to trace that number you gave us. Maybe it'll turn up something."

The uniformed officer closed his pad. "For now I recommend that you all head home and wait for a call from your friend Josh—or from his kidnappers."

A steady drizzle soaked the Jeep's windshield as they made their way back to the Takemura house. Nancy, Bess, and George stayed awake in their beds talking until well past midnight, discussing Josh's disappearance.

Finally Bess and George fell into a restless, fitful slumber. A keen sense of urgency kept Nancy awake long past the time that the other two girls were breathing steadily. She had to figure out what happened to Josh, and fast. Otherwise, their friend's life could be in serious danger!

The next morning Nancy was up before sunrise. As if her mind had continued working to solve the case while she was asleep, she was jolted awake by a sudden thought. Snake's note!

"George, Bess!" She shook the other two girls by the shoulders to wake them up.

"Huh?" George protested sleepily.

"Listen—what if the name *Cutter* on the note I found in Snake's pocket wasn't the name of a boat," Nancy said urgently. "What if Cutter is a name of a person?"

"Do you think Cutter could be Snake's name?" George had snapped awake.

"Maybe, George," Nancy replied. "It's a long shot, but let's just see if there are any Cutters listed in the phone book." She rummaged around the room for a telephone book.

Bess already had her hand on the receiver. "I have a better idea," she said, punching in the numbers 411. "Let's ask Information for the number."

Information had one listing for a T. Cutter. There was an address listed.

"Let's go check it out," Nancy said. She

turned to George. "I know you're not going to like this, but I think you should stay here," she said.

"What?—" George began.

"First of all, you need your rest." Nancy interrupted her friend's protest. "And second, we need you to stay by the phone in case Josh has been kidnapped—or in case we call and need your help."

"That makes sense," George said. "I admit I am a bit tired," she added as she got back under the covers.

Nancy and Bess dressed quickly, then woke Danny.

The leading edge of the storm had brought dark gray clouds that moved across the sky as they headed out in the Jeep.

"On the way, let's stop off at the beach to check to see what's up with the surfing contest," Nancy said.

A few fat, heavy raindrops pattered against the windshield. Danny peered up at the clouds. "Looks like the storm is finally starting to move in," he said.

The threesome drove in silence. They could feel the Jeep being buffeted by a strong wind that had kicked up from the east. "Looks pretty bad over that way," Danny said. "I'll bet the contest organizers will postpone the contest."

When they arrived at Honolua Beach, the pier area was almost deserted. Manny Monolo was running a storm flag up the pole at the end of the pier. The flag had a hollow swirl on it—the international symbol for a tropical storm.

"Contest's been postponed," Manny shouted to Danny over the sound of the rising surf. "The storm gained strength overnight, and it's supposed to hit the island at high tide in a couple of hours."

"That's great news!" Danny exclaimed. "Nobody would wish a storm on us," he added hastily, "but at least Josh won't lose his place in the standings while we're out searching for him."

Using a map from the glove compartment as well as Danny's knowledge of the island, they arrived at the area that Information had listed as the address for T. Cutter. The address was in a neighborhood on the fringes of a run-down harbor town called Point Guerre.

This town is the opposite of the beautiful seaside port of Lahaina, Nancy thought. Point Guerre was an industrial fishing and cannery town. The heavy smell of rotting fish hung everywhere.

The rain and blackening clouds had emptied the streets, making the town look dark and sinister. A group of rough-looking men standing out under an awning stared at Nancy and her friends as they cruised past in their Jeep.

"This place is no tourist town," Bess observed. "In fact, this whole area is kind of creepy."

Danny nodded. "Even an island paradise like Maui has its eyesores. Point Guerre is one of them. It has a pretty rowdy reputation."

They turned off the main street onto their destination, Kelton Way. This street was barely more than an alleyway, strewn with uncollected garbage. In one of the driveways, an abandoned car had been stripped.

Bess's face betrayed her apprehension as she took in their surroundings. "Whoever this T. Cutter is, he doesn't live too well," she said nervously. "I don't like this place," she added. "I hope this guy's not upset by our dropping in like this."

"You could wait in the car while I go check it out, Bess," Nancy told her. "In fact—Danny, why don't you stay with Bess so that she feels safer."

"Sure thing," Danny replied.

Danny pulled the car up in front of a block of sagging wooden row houses. The dilapidated houses looked like they hadn't been painted for years. Danny peered at the doorway of one of the houses. "That's One-oh-five Kelton, the number we're looking for," he said.

"Be right back," Nancy said, opening the car door. She got out of the car and knocked on the front door. There was no answer. After a moment Nancy knocked again, louder this time. She pushed open the door slightly—it wasn't locked.

"Mr. or Mrs. Cutter? T. Cutter?" Nancy called out. She pushed the door open all the way and peered into the dimly lit foyer. Along the right wall, a narrow staircase rose steeply to the second floor.

The house was silent. Nancy took a step farther inside. "Mr. Cutter?" she called out again. Again, no reply.

Nancy continued moving down the hall until she reached the kitchen doorway. As she stepped onto the kitchen floor, Nancy felt her shoe bump against something solid. She looked down, and felt a shock run through her like a bolt of electricity.

A man was sprawled facedown across the tiled kitchen floor. Lying next to him on the floor was a knife and a tiny trail of blood. The man had a twisted snake tattoo on his arm.

"It's the Snake," Nancy cried out loud. "And he's been stabbed!"

12

Out Cold

Nancy knelt beside the Snake, picked up his wrist, and felt a faint pulse. Then she ran to the front door to signal Danny and Bess to come inside.

Bess's jaw dropped at the sight of the Snake lying on the floor. "It *is* the Snake." The color drained from her face. "Is . . . is he still alive?"

Nancy nodded her head. "Yes, but just barely," she said. "We've got to get an ambulance here," she said, frantically looking around for a telephone.

After she had given the emergency operator all the information, Nancy looked around the room.

The kitchen floor right around the Snake's body showed heavy black scuff marks.

"From the way the knife is lying next to him and these scuff marks, I'd say he was stabbed while fighting with someone. These are definite signs of a struggle."

She noticed some objects scattered on the floor near where the Snake lay. There were a few loose coins, a pen, and a couple of wadded-up tissues. The tissues were streaked with traces of a glittery substance, Nancy noticed.

"Well, we know that Snake's real name must be T. Cutter, for starters—" Nancy began.

Nancy's thoughts were interrupted by the wailing of emergency sirens approaching from a distance.

"Timothy P. Cutter," the investigating officer read the name on the driver's license he'd just pulled from the Snake's pocket wallet. "We'll run a check on that name."

By now the kitchen was filled with police and emergency medical people.

Sergeant Danko had just arrived. He and the ranking lieutenant spoke with Nancy and her friends while the police technicians concluded their examination of the scene. The lieutenant was the same officer who was leading the investigation into Josh's disappearance.

"The Snake—I mean Cutter—was stabbed, wasn't he?" Nancy asked the policemen.

The lieutenant nodded. "That's correct. It looks like Cutter was stabbed once. He and the person who stabbed him were probably fighting over the knife. We'll take the weapon and examine it for fingerprints."

"What about checking Cutter's phone records?" Nancy asked them. "Phone records might provide a history of who he talked with recently. Maybe that would lead us to the person who is holding Josh."

"Good thinking, Nancy." Sergeant Danko looked at her admiringly. "You have a real detective's mind."

The lieutenant made some notes in his pad. "We'll certainly pursue those phone records, Ms. Drew, but it'll take a while to trace down the numbers," he explained.

Nancy was keenly aware that precious time was passing. Whoever stabbed Cutter had raised the stakes enormously. Cutter's attacker might be feeling panicked over his actions right now, and if Josh had been kidnapped, his situation could be all the more dangerous.

"What about that marine telephone number that was written on the note we found in Cutter's jacket?" she asked Danko. "Were you able to track that down?"

Danko nodded. "Yes, we did. The number was originally assigned to a boat registered out of Daring Harbor. The number isn't working anymore, though. And no owner is listed. I'm sorry it didn't turn up anything, Nancy," he said.

Nancy pressed her lips together. She felt frustrated by the missing link between Josh's disappearance and Cutter's attack. The only link so far was Cutter himself, and now, there was no telling if she'd be able to talk to Cutter.

An officer approached them. "Headquarters ran that check on Cutter you asked for, Lieutenant," he said. "Timothy Cutter is a small-time con, it turns out. His last permanent address was in Sydney, Australia, where the local authorities ran him out for petty theft, fraud, and trafficking protected animals. We have a line on him because he has already been busted several times in Honolulu."

"Sounds like Cutter is a real three-time loser," the lieutenant commented.

"You say he sold protected animals? Like birds and reptiles?" Nancy asked the officer.

The man nodded.

Nancy turned to Bess and Danny. "That might explain where that snake came from that was put in Josh's duffel bag. The death adder is native to Australia."

Danny nodded. "It fits together perfectly if Cutter recently moved here from Sydney."

The emergency medical team placed the wounded and unconscious Cutter on a stretcher and carried him out to the ambulance. The police began wrapping up their work at the scene. Nancy knew it served no further purpose for her and her friends to stay, so they prepared to return to the car.

"We'll keep you posted on everything that develops—especially if Cutter comes to," Danko promised them before they left. He glanced out the window. Sheets of rain were coming down. "And be careful driving out there. That storm outside is getting pretty bad."

A downpour soaked the group as they ran back to the Jeep. Water from the runoff was already creating a swirling mess of muddy streams on the streets of Point Guerre. "Good thing we have a four-wheel drive," Danny observed. "This is a really great vehicle to have in a storm."

They continued across the outer perimeter of Point Guerre and passed a big shopping complex. Nancy looked around. "Danny, could you pull into this parking lot?" she asked suddenly.

Danny turned the car into a grocery store parking lot. "What is it, Nancy?" he asked her. "You need to pick up something?"

"Not at all," Nancy replied. "I want us to retrace our steps and recall everything that's happened over the past few days. Maybe we've missed some important clue that will lead us to Josh."

"That sounds good," Bess said. She leaned forward from the backseat. "How do we start?" she asked.

"Let's start with a key question," Nancy said. "That is—how did Cutter know we were going snorkeling at Shipwreck Reef on Thursday? That's when he tried that shark-chumming stunt that scared us all so much. He must have found out where we were going somehow."

"Maybe he was following us at a distance the whole time," Bess suggested.

Nancy shook her head. "Maybe, but I was being very careful to watch for someone tailing us that day. Did anyone know where we were headed that day?"

"Let's see," Danny said thoughtfully. "After we found the threatening note, we picked up Josh and stopped at Ruby's Place to pick up snorkeling supplies."

"Right, and we ran into Hank Carter," Bess said. "But I don't remember anyone telling him about where we were going that day."

"Nor do I," Nancy said. "I questioned him a little later, and I didn't say anything then, I'm sure." She paused, considering. "What about while we were picking up our snorkeling supplies?" she asked.

"I might have said something about Shipwreck Reef to Neal, Ruby's clerk," Danny replied slowly. "Or maybe it was Ruby herself. I just can't remember exactly." He sighed.

"And later on I talked to Ruby in her office," Nancy continued. "We just talked about her surfing days, her friendship with Hank, and then she showed me one of her best-sellers, some kind of surfboard wax that was all glittery."

Nancy paused. "Hold on a minute," she said. "I just remembered something."

"What is it, Nancy?" Bess asked.

"Let's fast forward to the scene in Cutter's apartment," Nancy said quickly. "That stuff that was scattered around Cutter's body, Bess. What did we see there?"

Bess thought about Nancy's question. "Well," she began, "there was some loose change, some used tissues, and other stuff—you know, like someone spilled a purse."

"Like someone spilled a purse. You got it, Bess!" Nancy's voice rose excitedly. "It was right in front of us."

Nancy looked at Danny. "Danny, where does Ruby Blackwell live?"

"She lives on a houseboat near a small peninsula," Danny replied. "It's pretty remote—I think she likes her privacy. It's just east of Daring Harbor."

"Daring Harbor—that's where Sergeant Danko said that marine number had originally been registered—you remember, the number we found in Cutter's pocket," Nancy said.

"Daring Harbor—that's right!" Now Danny was getting excited, too. "And the boat that the number belonged to must be . . ."

"A houseboat." Nancy completed Danny's sentence. "Ruby Blackwell's houseboat, that is. I'll bet anything that the number in Cutter's jacket belonged to Ruby's houseboat."

"What does that mean?" Bess asked.

Nancy reached over the backseat and gave Bess a hug. "That means we may be a step closer to finding Josh. I think Ruby may have kidnapped Josh. She may have even stabbed Cutter!"

13

The Calm Before the Storm

Bess looked aghast at Nancy's statement. "You think Ruby Blackwell kidnapped Josh and tried to kill Cutter? Why?"

"I don't have all the pieces put together yet, but I'll fill you in on my thinking in just a minute," Nancy replied. "I know the weather's bad, Danny, but let's head over to Ruby's place. I want to take a look around."

"Sure thing," Danny replied, starting the engine. "I know where she used to keep her houseboat anchored. With any luck, it's still there."

"Great," Nancy said. She reached for the car door. "But first we need to call George and tell her where we're going."

Danny pulled up to the front of the store.

Nancy ran into the grocery store to find a pay phone. She had to struggle against the stiff wind to open the door.

She found a phone just inside the store. Just as she dropped some coins into the slot, a loud clap of thunder crashed overhead. The lights in the store flickered for a moment.

George answered the call quickly. "George," Nancy said urgently. "I don't have much time to explain. The Snake has been stabbed. He's unconscious and was taken to the hospital. We think Ruby may be behind it."

"Ruby Blackwell?" George sounded shocked. "How can that be?"

"I can't explain right now, but she may have kidnapped Josh." Nancy's words were hurried. "We're heading over to her houseboat right now. It's anchored near Daring Harbor. I want you to—"

Nancy was cut off midsentence by another deafening crack of thunder, followed by a burst of lightning. The grocery store's lights flickered, and then went dark.

"George?" Nancy spoke into the receiver. "George!"

It was no use—the line was dead. The storm must have knocked out the telephone lines as well as the electricity. Nancy realized that she had been cut off before she'd had a chance to tell

George to have the police meet them at Ruby's address.

Outside, the rain was hitting the pavement so hard that it bounced up off the ground. Nancy returned to the Jeep and shut the door, thankful to be back inside and out of the rain and wind.

"Nancy, what makes you suspect that it was Ruby who stabbed Cutter?" Danny asked as he nosed the Jeep onto the rain-slick street.

"Remember those tissues on the floor next to Cutter's body?" Nancy reminded them.

Danny nodded.

"They were streaked with traces of glittering pink wax. That's the custom surfboard wax that Ruby mixes and sells in her shop. She told me herself that she's always having to wipe it off her hands with tissue."

"So, the fact that those tissues with the surfboard wax were next to Cutter—" Danny began.

"Means that Ruby must have been with Cutter when he was stabbed," Nancy concluded. "What I don't know is why she was with Cutter. Maybe she was working with him and they had a falling out, or maybe he was blackmailing her for some reason. She could even have stabbed him."

"It's all so hard to believe." Bess shook her head. "Ruby seems so nice."

Nancy nodded. "I know what you mean, Bess. I remember overhearing a call that sounded like someone was threatening her—maybe that was Cutter."

"You said you also think she kidnapped Josh?" Bess asked.

Nancy shook her head. "I don't have the answer for that, yet. But I suspect it has something to do with her financial woes and her contract with Golf Coast. We know she's been short of cash. She's borrowed money, sold her ruby ring, and has a big pile of overdue bills. There must be some financial reason that she wanted Josh out of the contest."

"I hope the road to the harbor hasn't washed out," Danny said, shifting the car into first gear. "If so, you can only approach that area by boat."

"And this is certainly no day for a boat ride," Bess said. "Listen to the rain pounding on the car's roof."

By now they had been driving down the main beach highway for about thirty minutes. Danny slowed the car down next to a prominent cluster of sandalwood trees. He peered at the opening to a side road.

"There's no sign, but I recognize those trees. This must be it—Daring Way." He turned off the highway onto the road, which was barely more than two muddy strips cutting through the tropical forest.

Danny shifted the Jeep into low gear and edged the vehicle forward. Even at slow speed, it was a bumpy ride.

"Whoa, this is wilder than an amusement park ride," Bess said.

They reached the end of Daring Way. The road stopped at a pebbly beach that had a wooden ramp leading down into the water. The beach overlooked a small harbor. They could see a squat, boxy houseboat anchored about fifty yards offshore.

"There. That's Ruby's boat," Danny said, pointing to the vessel. "Her dinghy is tied up to the landing here—we can use it to reach the boat."

"Hey, you two." Bess nudged Nancy with her elbow. "In case you've forgotten, there's a wicked tropical storm out there. We'll tip over."

"We'll make it, Bess," Nancy assured her. "But you can stay here if you prefer."

Bess looked around her, as if weighing her options. None seemed pleasing. "All right," she said grudgingly. "Count me in."

The three got into the dinghy and cast off. Nancy paddled at the bow, Danny at the stern. Bess sat on the floor in the middle of the little boat, her head bent against the weather. She clutched the dinghy's sides for dear life.

Fortunately, the wind was behind them, and they quickly made their way across the roiling waters to Ruby's houseboat.

As they pulled up to the houseboat, Nancy cast a line around a guardrail and pulled them the rest of the way in. The houseboat looked dark and deserted. There was no sign of anyone around.

The troubled sea was causing the houseboat to pitch and roll with the waves. "Make sure you keep hold of something while you're walking out here," Nancy warned the other two. "We don't want anyone to fall overboard."

"Ooh, my stomach," Bess said as Danny helped her climb out of the dinghy and onto the deck. "Call me a landlubber, but I think living on a boat is completely nuts."

Nancy edged her way around the perimeter of the houseboat and peeked into a darkened window. She saw no sign of anyone.

She reported the information to her friends. "I thought I saw a glimmer of light coming from the forward cabin, though," she said. She pushed open a side door. Quietly Nancy stole into the houseboat, followed closely by Bess and Danny.

Nancy was heading toward a thin strip of light that was coming from under the door of the forward cabin. She reached the door and tried the handle. It was locked.

Suddenly she heard a muffled cry coming from the other side of the locked door. The voice sounded familiar.

"That could be Josh!" Bess cried out. "Quick, Nancy! Open the door!"

"I'll try," Nancy replied. She reached into her pocket and took out a plastic identification card. She wedged the card between the lock and the door frame, and worked it back and forth. Fortunately, the lock was flimsy, and it gave way after a minute.

Nancy opened the door, and the three looked inside.

"Josh!" Bess gasped.

Josh was lying on his side across a bunk, bound and gagged. Josh's eyes widened when he saw Nancy, Bess, and Danny burst through the door.

Nancy rushed over to Josh and quickly removed the gag from his mouth. "Nancy . . ." Josh's voice cracked with dryness from having been gagged.

"Josh." Bess's voice quavered. "Are you okay? I was so afraid that something terrible had happened to you."

"I'm okay," Josh said weakly. He reached out for Bess's hand.

"What happened, Josh? Who brought you here? Was it the Snake?" Nancy asked him.

Josh nodded. "He waylaid me somehow inside

the restaurant—I think he had a cloth soaked with some kind of knockout drug. Next thing I knew, I woke up here. I haven't seen anyone else."

Nancy noticed a strong odor of some kind of fuel wafting through the room. She didn't know where the odor was coming from, but she knew they'd better get out of there quickly. She explained what had happened over the past few hours. "Timothy Cutter is the real name of the man we were calling the Snake. He's wounded—someone stabbed him."

Josh gave a low whistle. "Pardon my saying so, but it couldn't have happened to a nicer guy. Where are we—what boat is this?"

"You're on Ruby Blackwell's houseboat," Nancy told him.

"Ruby? What's she got to do with all this?" Josh sounded confused.

"Josh, you don't know how truly sorry I am that you'll have to find out the answer to that question." A shaky-sounding voice came from somewhere behind them.

Then Nancy felt some kind of liquid splash across her clothing. She turned around to see Ruby Blackwell standing in the doorway. In one hand, she was holding a bottle filled with the liquid that she had just splashed on Nancy. In the other hand, she was holding a plastic lighter.

Ruby's normally beautiful face appeared altered, Nancy noticed. Her expression was desperate, like that of a cornered animal.

Nancy took a step toward Ruby.

Ruby backed up and flicked the lighter. "Not so fast, Nancy," she said. "That's kerosene I just soaked you with. One touch of this flame and you'll go up like a Molotov cocktail."

Nancy touched her shirt with her hand, then sniffed her fingers. Ruby was telling the truth—her shirt was covered with kerosene. The smell of the fuel permeated the room.

"I mean business, Nancy," Ruby said flatly. "While you were all in here rescuing Josh, I soaked the deck with kerosene. Don't come any closer, or you'll be the first to die!"

14

A Desperate Act

Nancy was focused on the wild look in Ruby's eyes. The young woman was desperate enough to try something crazy. Anything Nancy tried at this point might rattle Ruby and set off an explosion.

Nancy decided to try to stall for time in the hope that George had figured out that Nancy had wanted her to contact the police.

"We've found Josh, Ruby, so you can let us go now," she said slowly.

"Don't think I'm stupid!" Ruby snapped. She jerked her arms, waving the flame dangerously close to the gas-soaked rag. "I can't let you all go. I'm in too deep as it is."

"Why, Ruby?" Josh spoke up. "What started all of this?"

Ruby remained silent. She started rocking back and forth on her heels and waving the lighter—as if she was building up to some kind of action, Nancy thought grimly.

Nancy knew she needed to keep Ruby talking in order for them to stay alive. "I know what happened—you needed money, didn't you?" she began. "And the Golf Coast Surf-Off was your big chance. Tell me, Ruby. Was Hank Carter going to give you his winnings if something happened to Josh?"

Ruby looked at Nancy. "You've almost got it figured, Nancy. Yes, I wanted to get money from the contest, but not in the way you think. The Golf Coast contest is my big chance to launch my surfboard, the Stinger. Golf Coast is going to market it all over the world."

Nancy thought about the conversation she'd overheard earlier between Ruby and the Golf Coast executive. They had been arguing over a marketing and promotions contract.

Suddenly it all began to make sense. "I see. So, they'll market the Stinger, but only if Hank wins the contest this week, is that right?" she asked.

Ruby nodded. "Josh, you know I tried to get you to go with the Stinger, too, but you wouldn't," she said crossly. "You blew it for all of us."

"But, Ruby—" Josh began.

Nancy motioned for Josh to stop talking. Ruby was making less and less sense, and Nancy didn't want Josh to push her over the edge.

"So tell me, Ruby," Nancy continued. "How did you meet Timothy Cutter?"

Ruby gave a chilling smile. "Oh, yes. Cutter—you all called him the Snake. He and I had a good laugh about that one." She looked at Nancy. "My good old friend Captain Russell Frye gave me Cutter's name as someone who would do a job, without asking questions. Russell had no idea what I was planning to do, though."

"So, you hired Cutter to steal Josh's surfboard?" Nancy prompted her.

Ruby nodded. "That was all I really wanted from Josh—to get his board so that he would take me up on my offer to ride the Stinger and win the contest with it."

"Then what went wrong? Why all the threats and attacks? And why the attempt on Cutter's life?" Nancy asked.

"Cutter got an idea of how much money I stood to make from the Golf Coast contract, and he started blackmailing me," Ruby explained. "I wanted him to stop."

She looked at Josh. "Cutter kept doing worse and worse things. He said he'd tell the police that *I* did them, and he'd skip the country. Then I'd end up taking the fall," she said.

"So you went to Cutter's house to confront him," Nancy suggested.

Ruby's chest heaved. "Yes, I tried to argue with him. I even threatened to turn the tables and turn him in," she explained. "That's when he started waving around that knife. I got scared and fought with him, and the knife fell to the floor. We both grabbed for it. I got there first. Then he lunged for me. And I guess you know the rest. I still can't believe I stabbed him. He shouldn't have come at me so hard, or he'd still be alive. It was all his fault."

Nancy realized that Ruby thought the knife wound had been fatal. Of course, she thought. She had left him for dead.

"I killed him," Ruby snarled. "Just like I'm going to kill you."

Nancy felt a cold bead of sweat pop out on her brow. "You're no murderer, Ruby. You didn't kill Cutter. He was wounded, and he's in the hospital. The police will understand why you stabbed him."

"No, no!" The wild expression returned to Ruby's eyes. "I'm ruined, can't you see? The stabbing, the kidnapping, the stuff Cutter did—no one can ever know about any of that, or I'm finished!"

"So you'll kill us all? I can't believe that, Ruby," Nancy said soothingly. "You're not like that."

For a second Nancy thought her words might be having an effect on Ruby. The surf shop owner blinked and lowered the lighter slightly. Then she snapped back to an angry expression.

"No, it's too late." Ruby shook her head. "I can't let everything I've worked for go down the drain. I want you all on the stern. Now!" she ordered.

Nancy and the others were forced to follow Ruby onto the rear deck of the houseboat.

"Tell me something, Ruby," Nancy said as they made their way through the houseboat. "Were you also behind what happened to those other two surfers, Jo Jo Sergeant and Keiko Mann?"

Ruby shook her head. "Keiko managed to come down with food poisoning all on his own. But his illness did give me the idea to drive the top competitors away from the contest. Cutter planted the skateboard that tripped Jo Jo, and next on the list was Josh."

The houseboat gave a sudden lurch in the storm. Nancy was too far away from Ruby to make her move, but she started positioning herself closer to knock away the lighter.

They arrived on the back deck. To Nancy's surprise, they came face-to-face with Hank Carter. Hank was just climbing onboard from a motorized skiff.

"What's going on here?" Hank demanded. "Ruby?" he asked. Nancy could see that he looked confused by the sight of Ruby holding the lighter. "I came to check to make sure you were all right in the storm."

"Hank, you shouldn't have come," Ruby said. "Now everything is ruined."

"What's ruined? What are you talking about? And what are you doing with that kerosene?"

"You're going to win the contest, Hank, don't you see?" The slightly mad, singsong quality had returned to Ruby's voice. "These people are all going to disappear, and you and I will win that contest and be together forever."

Hank took a deep breath. "Ruby, you know I care. And I want to win that contest as much as anyone. But this is crazy!" He raised his hands in a gesture of helplessness.

Ruby stared wildly at Hank. The lighter flame inched closer to the kerosene bucket. "You take that back!" she yelled. "It's not crazy—I did this for you as well as me!" Her voice took on a determined, deadly tone. "Climb back in your boat, Hank."

Looking scared, Hank did as Ruby said. Ruby prepared to lower herself into the boat next to Hank. Just then she accidentally dropped the lighter. It fell onto her skirt. The garment instantly burst into flame.

Before Ruby had a chance to cry out, Nancy tackled her. The two of them were thrown into the water by the force of Nancy's attack.

Nancy dived under the waves. She kicked hard to rise to the surface, coughing and gasping for air.

"Nancy! Take my hand!" Josh yelled to her.

Hank had dived overboard to grab Ruby. Just then, Nancy could see pulsing blue lights strobing out to them from the shore. She breathed a sigh of relief—the police had finally arrived.

15

Aloha

"Ahh, there's nothing like the calm after the storm." Danny inhaled deeply and smiled at Nancy. "Don't you agree?"

"You mean the calm after two storms, don't you, Danny?" Nancy said with a wry half-smile. "That is, yesterday's tropical storm, and 'Hurricane Ruby.'" She leaned forward and rested her arms on the wooden railing of the pier at Honolua Beach.

They were standing with George and Bess at the far end of the pier, watching the finals of the Golf Coast Surf-Off. The tropical storm from the previous day had moved on past the island, leaving a glorious sapphire sky in its wake.

Danny shook his head. "It seems almost like a

bad dream now—how Ruby turned on us yesterday. And to think that all along she was trying to scare Josh away from the contest!"

"Well, Josh is certainly making up for his lost momentum today," George observed. Josh had returned in triumph to today's surfing finals. To no one's surprise, his scores so far put him way out in front of the pack, trailed by Hank Carter.

"What do you think will happen to Ruby, now that she's been busted for what she did?" Bess asked them.

"For starters, I expect she'll be in the hospital for a few days, recovering from those kerosene burns," Nancy replied. "Fortunately, none of the burns was serious. After that, it'll be up to the local authorities to decide what to do with her."

"And get this, you guys," Danny nudged Nancy with his elbow. "Hank Carter has hired some kind of big-time lawyer to take her case. He wants to make sure she's well represented."

"I can't believe that Hank remains so loyal to Ruby, after all that she did," Nancy said. "That'll really make Marisa jealous!"

Josh had just cruised to shore on his final surfing run. After a moment the judges raised their score cards. The scores revealed that Josh had won the contest by a wide margin.

"Yes!" Danny yelped happily, pumping his fist

into the air. "I can just see the headline on tomorrow's sports page: 'Josh-man Nails the Golf Coast.'"

"Presenting this award and a check for seventy-five thousand dollars to . . . Josh Brightman!"

Cameras flashed and TV crews moved in for close-ups as Josh bounded up the steps of the judge's stand to accept his prize.

"Hey, Josh! How about an interview?" The local TV sports reporter called to him.

"In just a minute," Josh replied with a big grin. He walked over to the spot where Danny, Nancy, Bess, and George were standing.

Ignoring the people mobbing him with congratulations and requests for autographs, Josh swooped Bess off her feet into his arms and gave her a big hug. Another camera flash went off. "Hey, that's tomorrow's feature picture for the sports page!" a reporter laughingly announced.

"Hey, Josh," a low voice sounded behind Josh. The voice belonged to Manny Monolo. The lifeguard awkwardly stuck out his hand.

"Big congratulations on your win, Josh," Manny said. He shifted uncomfortably on his feet, then added, "And I wanted to say I'm sorry I've been kind of chilly toward you since last summer. I was out of line."

145

"No hard feelings, Manny." Josh's reply was warm and friendly.

Manny returned Josh's smile. "I've reapplied to the paramedic program for next year. They've agreed to take me on a trial basis next spring. So, it looks like I get another shot."

"That's terrific, Manny!" George exclaimed "You'll make a great paramedic—I know it."

"Will you look at that . . ." Danny interrupted them. He was staring out toward the bay, using his hand to shield against the sun's glare. "I do not believe what I'm seeing!" Danny exclaimed.

Nancy turned and looked in the direction that Danny was pointing. Captain Frye's boat was steaming across the bay with a load of tourists. The shark painting, however, was gone from the side of the ship. Instead, the entire vessel had been redecorated as a pirate ship, complete with fake cannons and square rigging. The advertising sign displayed on the bow had been changed to read "Cap'n Frye's Authentic Pirate Tour!"

"Frye must have given up on the shark-chumming business and turned pirate," Nancy said. She was amused to see that the crew and Frye himself were decked out in pirate costumes. "One thing is sure—Frye sure makes one cranky-looking pirate captain!" she added, laughing at the glum-faced Frye.

"Seems like the perfect business for him." Josh

grinned. "One thing you can say about Frye—he's always got an angle."

Josh was holding his arm around a beaming Bess. In the other hand, he held the shiny first place surfing trophy.

"You should really have this trophy, Nancy," he said, offering the statue to her. "Without you, I wouldn't even be here. I owe you a big load of thanks."

Nancy held up her hands and laughingly refused the prize. "Thanks a lot, Josh. But I don't deserve this at all," she said. "One thing I would like, though," she added, her eyes sparkling, "is an invitation back. Because after this week in Maui, I need one very relaxing vacation."

"You can say that again," George said. "The next time we hit the shores of Maui, it'll be for some real R and R."

"It's a deal," Danny said. "You know, *aloha* means both hello and goodbye in Hawaiian, so why don't we say aloha for now—and we'll see you back here soon."

"And since we're E-mail pen pals, I'll just say I'll 'E' you real soon," Nancy said to the happy groans of the rest of the group.

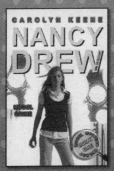

FRANKLIN W. DIXON

THE HARDY BOYS

Undercover Brothers®

INVESTIGATE THESE TWO ADVENTUROUS MYSTERY TRILOGIES WITH AGENTS FRANK AND JOE HARDY!

#25 Double Trouble

#26 Double Down

#28 Galaxy X

#29 X-plosion

#27 Double Deception

#30 The X-Factor

From Aladdin
Published by Simon & Schuster

PHYLLIS REYNOLDS NAYLOR

STARTING WITH ALICE
Atheneum Books for
  Young Readers
  0-689-84395-X
Aladdin Paperbacks
  0-689-84396-8

ALICE IN BLUNDERLAND
Atheneum Books for
  Young Readers
  0-689-84397-6
Aladdin Paperbacks
  0-689-84398-4

LOVINGLY ALICE
Atheneum Books for
  Young Readers
  0-689-84399-2
Aladdin Paperbacks
  0-689-84400-X

THE AGONY OF ALICE
Atheneum Books for
  Young Readers
  0-689-31143-5
Aladdin Paperbacks
  0-689-81672-3

ALICE IN RAPTURE,
  SORT-OF
Atheneum Books for
  Young Readers
  0-689-31466-3
Aladdin Paperbacks
  0-689-81687-1

RELUCTANTLY ALICE
Atheneum Books for
  Young Readers
  0-689-31681-X
Aladdin Paperbacks
  0-689-81688-X

ALL BUT ALICE
Atheneum Books for
Young Readers
  0-689-31773-5
Aladdin Paperbacks
  0-689-85044-1

ALICE IN APRIL
Atheneum Books for
  Young Readers
  0-689-31805-7
Aladdin Paperbacks
  0-689-81686-3

ALICE IN-BETWEEN
Atheneum Books for
  Young Readers
  0-689-31890-0
Aladdin Paperbacks
  0-689-81685-5

ALICE THE BRAVE
Atheneum Books for
  Young Readers
  0-689-80095-9
Aladdin Paperbacks
  0-689-80598-5

ALICE IN LACE
Atheneum Books for
  Young Readers
  0-689-80358-3
Aladdin Paperbacks
  0-689-80597-7

OUTRAGEOUSLY ALICE
Atheneum Books for
  Young Readers
  0-689-80354-0
Aladdin Paperbacks
  0-689-80596-9

ACHINGLY ALICE
Atheneum Books for
  Young Readers
  0-689-80533-9
Aladdin Paperbacks
  0-689-80595-0
Simon Pulse
  0-689-86396-9

ALICE ON THE OUTSIDE
Atheneum Books for
  Young Readers
  0-689-80359-1
Simon Pulse
  0-689-80594-2

GROOMING OF ALICE
Atheneum Books for
  Young Readers
  0-689-82633-8
Simon Pulse
  0-689-84618-5

ALICE ALONE
Atheneum Books for
  Young Readers
  0-689-82634-6
Simon Pulse
  0-689-85189-8

SIMPLY ALICE
Atheneum Books for
  Young Readers
  0-689-84751-3
Simon Pulse
  0-689-85965-1

PATIENTLY ALICE
Atheneum Books for
  Young Readers
  0-689-82636-2
Simon Pulse
  0-689-87073-6

INCLUDING ALICE
Atheneum Books for
  Young Readers
  0-689-82637-0
Simon Pulse
  0-689-87074-4

ALICE ON HER WAY
Atheneum Books for
  Young Readers
  0-689-87090-6

ALICE IN THE KNOW
Atheneum Books for
  Young Readers
  0-689-87092-2